'You can't stormed.

Her hands were knew it was only with difficulty she refrained from pummelling him.

'Do what, Steph?' he asked quietly.

'Come back into my life like this. Haunt me this way. Why, Harry? Why?'

She was so distressed he reached out and rested the back of his fingers, oh, so lightly, against her cheek.

'I would never do anything to hurt you, Steph, you must know that. And as for haunting you—I didn't know you were working in the clinic. Yes, I'd have contacted you, probably tomorrow or the next day. I wanted to see you...'

There—he'd said it.

Previously a teacher, shopkeeper, travel agent, pig farmer, builder and worker in the disability field (among other things), the 'writing bug' struck **Meredith Webber** unexpectedly. 'I entered a competition run by a women's magazine, shared the third prize with two hundred and fifty other would-be writers, and found myself infected. Thirty-something books later, I'm still suffering. Medical romances appeal to me because they offer the opportunity to include a wider cast of characters, and the challenge of interweaving a love story into the drama of medical or paramedical practice.'

Recent titles by the same author:

DAISY AND THE DOCTOR*
THE DOCTOR'S DESTINY*
DEAR DOCTOR*
DR GRAHAM'S MARRIAGE*

*The *Westside Stories* sequence

THE SURGEON'S SECOND CHANCE

BY
MEREDITH WEBBER

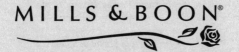

MILLS & BOON®

All the characters in this book have no existence outside the imagination of the author, and have no relation whatsoever to anyone bearing the same name or names. They are not even distantly inspired by any individual known or unknown to the author, and all the incidents are pure invention.

First published in Great Britain 2003
Harlequin Mills & Boon Limited,
Eton House, 18-24 Paradise Road, Richmond, Surrey TW9 1SR

© Meredith Webber 2003

ISBN 0 263 83448 4

Set in Times Roman 10½ on 12 pt.
03-0603-47667

Printed and bound in Spain
by Litografia Rosés, S.A., Barcelona

CHAPTER ONE

WITH an umbrella that was proving useless against the deluge from the heavens, Harry picked his way through the mud, slush and landscaping debris in front of the new hospital building, finally skidding to a halt in the sheltered entrance.

The wide glass doors slid efficiently open, and he entered the foyer, stepping carefully on mats spread over the thick plastic protecting the new carpet. Plastic pathways led in various directions, but he'd been told where to go and took the one leading to the left, which fetched up at a door marked CHIEF ADMINISTRATOR'S OFFICE.

The man who bade him enter wasn't the new chief administrator but the real power behind the hospital— the man who'd built and owned it, Bob Quayle.

'Harry! Good to see you, my boy!'

Bob, smooth, sleek and silver-haired, rose from behind the desk, and came around it, hand outstretched, to shake Harry's, then throw a friendly arm around his shoulders.

'So, you've finally returned to the best country in the world, and rumour has it you'll soon be the most sought-after plastic surgeon in Queensland.'

'I don't know where you heard that rumour, Bob.' Harry deflected the praise with ease. 'Starting up a practice takes time. I have to meet and gain the confidence of the local GPs for referrals, and to do whatever public hospital work I can get, so my name becomes known in the local profession.'

'Ah, but once people know you've exclusive rights to practise in the newest, most up-to-date private hospital in the whole south-east region, you'll have referrals flocking in,' Bob assured him. 'Summerland's become more than a holiday destination these days, it's one of the fastest-growing cities in the state. And with more and more wealthy people retiring to the new secured estates along the ocean front, you'll have a continual flow of potential customers.'

Harry thought of explaining, again, to Bob that elective cosmetic surgery was only a very small part of his work, but, knowing the older man wouldn't listen, he swallowed the protest.

'The thing is,' Bob continued, 'as you saw when you came in, the rain has set us back a few weeks.'

He hesitated, then said, 'It will be a month before anyone can start work in the new specialists' suites, and probably some weeks after that before the hospital becomes fully operational.'

Harry wasn't surprised by this news. He'd guessed it was why Bob had asked to see him.

'That's OK with me,' he assured the older man. 'I've only been back in the country a couple of days and I need to find a flat, unpack, then organise furniture, equipment and staff for the rooms. A month's delay won't bother me at all.'

'Well, maybe I can help you with the flat,' Bob said expansively. 'I've a couple of apartments I keep for visiting friends and relations—all furnished, of course. Why don't you take one of them for, say, three months? That'd give you time to get to know the place a bit better and decide where you might eventually like to live.'

Harry studied his benefactor. Although he didn't

know Bob Quayle the businessman all that well, instinct told him this man didn't give much away.

But accepting the offer would save him looking for a place—and finding furniture—and he couldn't think of any really impossible strings Bob might attach to the offer.

'Sounds good. I'd be happy to pay rent,' he said, but Bob waved his offer away.

'Nonsense! I think of you as family—you know that!' he said, his voice suddenly gruff.

Does he? Harry wondered, thinking of the man's real family—his son, Martin, who'd been one of Harry's two best friends at university. He and Martin and Steph—a tightly bound threesome from the time they'd met in a lecture theatre on the first day of their medical course, when their surnames had linked them into a study group...

'Besides, you could do me a favour at the same time.'

Bob paused and looked directly at Harry.

'One good turn deserves another and all that. I don't mean the flat, that's nothing, but the bed you negotiated as part of your tenancy at the hospital. I'm still not sure how you talked me into that.'

Harry shifted uneasily. When he'd first asked Bob about the possibility of the free use of a theatre and an occasional free bed in the new hospital, Bob had seen the potential of the good publicity special charity cases could generate, but it had still been a struggle to convince him it was worth agreeing.

Was this payback time?

'The apartment I have in mind for you is on the twelfth floor of Dolphin Towers,' Bob continued smoothly—certain he'd got his message across. 'It's one of the first buildings I built in Summerland, on the main road in the centre of the tourist strip. There are shops and offices on the first three levels, and a twenty-four-hour medical clinic, catering mainly to tourists, on the ground floor.'

He paused and his keen grey eyes studied Harry for a minute.

'It's the clinic where you could do me a favour. It ran into a bit of financial trouble recently, and I ended up buying out the owner. My accountants assure me it should be a viable concern, but though they're clued-up about hospitals now, they know nothing about how medical practices run. I wondered, as you'll be without rooms to practise from for a month, if you'd mind taking a look at the clinic for me. Maybe spend a couple of days there so you get a feel for the place and see how it works—staff rosters, patient flow-through, things like that. I'd pay you, of course, and throw in the apartment.'

Ah! Harry thought as the words confirmed his instinct that Bob Quayle gave little away.

But with a furnished flat provided while he settled into the holiday city, he *would* have time on his hands...

'I'd like to help out, Bob,' he said, 'but it's years since I've done any general practice, and—'

'But I don't want you doing medical work,' Bob broke in before Harry had properly organised his thoughts. 'Just take a look at how it's operating. There's a part-time office manager you can talk to, and a desk in her office you could use. You're a clever man, you can't deny that. And you did work shifts in twenty-four-hour clinics when you first graduated and were saving money to go overseas. You should be able to see where things are going wrong. Discreetly, of course. It's not public knowledge I'm the new owner, and I'd like to keep it that way. Especially with the staff.'

Harry ran the conversation over in his head, and though a niggling feeling of suspicion lingered deep in his subconscious—maybe because Martin had always talked about his father's devious streak—he could see no harm in granting the older man's wish.

'I guess I can take a look at things,' he said, 'though I can't promise you I'll find anything. Have you any ideas about its future yourself? Do you want to get into running medical practices as a sideline to private hospitals?'

Bob shook his head.

'To tell you the truth, it's a complication I don't need. But it's hard to lay off staff these days, with all the problems of workplace agreements and contracts. I guess if I can prove it's not viable, it would give me a reason to close it.'

Harry nodded. That sounded much more like the canny—probably greedy—businessman he guessed Bob to be. The space could probably be used for something that would bring Bob in a lot more money.

They talked a little longer—about the past, Harry's friendship with Martin, and about Doreen, Bob's wife, who'd suffered ill health since Martin's death. Then Bob gave him the phone number of his business manager, who would show Harry the apartment and the clinic, and generally help him get settled in.

As Harry squelched back through the mire at the front of the hospital, he wondered about the people who hadn't been mentioned in the conversation—about Steph and her daughter, Fanny.

Martin's daughter Fanny.

*   *   *

Stephanie Prince tucked her daughter into bed, and bent to kiss her on the forehead.

'Tell me the story of Daddy falling off the horse when you all went out to Uncle Harry's farm,' Fanny demanded.

Steph smiled at the little girl, and gently touched her cheek. Was it because Fanny had never known her father that stories of his deeds and exploits were far more interesting to her than fairy-tales?

'It was a long time ago,' she began, 'not long after Daddy, Uncle Harry and I first met.'

She'd told it so often the words came out automatically, while in her head she was remembering those days. She, Harry and Martin—brought together by the accident of surnames—Prince, Pritchard and Quayle. But against all odds, Martin, the spoilt darling of a wealthy family, she herself, the girl from the wrong side of the tracks, and Harry, who claimed he came from so far west there were no tracks, had become friends, and then an inseparable threesome.

In the later years of their medical course, clinical rotations had often separated them for months, and during their intern year they'd seen even less of each other. But the bond had always been there.

Until—

She shook off the shadows of the past, and concentrated on the story.

'So Daddy's sitting on this horse, and pretending he knows all about riding, when Uncle Harry flicked his fingers to his dog, and the dog barked right behind the horse's hooves. The horse reared up and Daddy, who'd got such a fright he'd let go of the reins, slid off the saddle and right back down over the horse's rump and tail and, bump, landed on his backside on the ground.'

Fanny, who at four thought backsides irrepressibly funny, laughed and laughed, and Steph, who'd been finding life far from funny lately, felt her heart swell with love for this darling daughter who was all that remained to her of that other, carefree, happy existence.

Except her surname, of course, which she'd determinedly kept for professional reasons back when she'd married Martin, and since his death had used solely for personal reasons...

'Now, off to sleep, Fanny mine,' she said, smoothing back the blonde curls from the small, flushed face. 'I'll see you in the morning.'

Fanny gave her a final hug, then, clutching the ragged bear who was her favoured bed-mate at the moment, turned over and closed her eyes.

She *is* secure, Stephanie reassured herself as she left the room. An insecure child wouldn't go off to sleep so happily.

But worry had been her constant companion lately, so the reassurance didn't do much to banish her guilt that in another hour she'd leave her sleeping child and go to work.

'You would hear her if she woke in the night, wouldn't you?' she asked, directing her question at the young girl who sat, head bowed over a book, in her living room.

Tracy looked up and grinned at her.

'Do you know, you ask me that every night?' she teased. 'And every night I tell you I would hear her. In fact, a week or so ago, she lost Adeline—you know, that incredibly ugly doll those grandparents gave her—out of bed and yelled for me to come and find her. She went straight back to sleep afterwards.'

Steph nodded, knowing Tracy was telling the truth but finding little comfort.

'Look,' Tracy said, with all the confidence of eighteen

years, 'your mother was a single parent and you turned out all right.'

'But my mother didn't go out to work. She worked from home. I should have been something I could do from home.'

Tracy sighed and Steph recovered a remnant of her sense of humour.

'I know,' she said, 'I'm obsessing. I'm sorry. Especially as it makes it seem as if I don't trust you.'

She reached over the back of the couch and gave her cousin a warm hug.

'You're the best thing that could possibly have happened to Fanny and me,' she said. 'I think it's just that I've worried for so long that now things seem to be working out, I keep waiting for something bad to happen.'

The foreboding hovered on the fringe of her conscious mind as she prepared for work, showering then shaking her super-short hair into place and pulling on jeans and a T-shirt, comfortable garb to wear under a white coat.

A final peep at Fanny, sound asleep, then she was off.

'See you in the morning,' she called to Tracy as she opened the back door, looked out at the flooding rain and sighed. Even with an umbrella, she'd be soaked by the time she reached the car. And then the aging vehicle, which hated wet weather, would probably refuse to start.

'One day!' she muttered to herself, looking up at the heavens where the planets ruling her life were surely permanently misaligned. 'One day my luck has to change!'

It did, in so far as the car started the first time, but when she reached the underground car park, the parking spaces designated for clinic staff were all full and she had to drive down into the bowels of the earth to find a vacant spot.

'You're late!' Rebecca, the clinic receptionist on night duty greeted her, and Steph glanced automatically at her watch.

Rebecca laughed.

'Honestly, Steph, you fall for that every time. But you are five minutes past your usual arrival time—only ten minutes early instead of fifteen.'

'Someone's pinched the parking spaces again,' Stephanie told her. 'I wish the guy who's supposed to clamp illegally parked cars would just once clamp the cars in those spaces.'

'Well, one's mine,' Rebecca said, 'and Peter's still here so his car is probably there, and Joanne's, and maybe the new bloke. That'd make four.'

'The new bloke? What new bloke? Don't tell me we're getting a second doctor for midweek night duty? Miracles do happen!'

'Yeah?' Rebecca's tone echoed her disbelief. 'I don't know that he's a doctor, just that Muriel left a message saying some new bloke's coming to check out the place. Succinct and informative as ever, our Muriel.'

Stephanie chuckled. She'd never met Muriel, the late-shift day receptionist at the clinic, but was aware she and Rebecca had a running battle over messages, charts, information-sharing and probably the number of spoons in the tearoom.

'But if he was here, you'd have seen him,' she pointed out.

Rebecca shrugged.

'Not necessarily. He could be hiding in the adminis-trator's room. No one's been in there at night since the clinic changed hands—and Flo's only been working part time for months.'

Steph nodded. Flo had been the full-time office manager, and had often worked in the evenings so she could keep an eye on things on the night shift, but her hours had been drastically reduced since the new owners had taken over.

'We could sneak the door open and have a look,' Steph suggested, but at that moment the front door opened and three young Japanese—two women and a man—came in, brushing rain off their jackets and looking around for somewhere to put their umbrellas.

Rebecca hurried out from behind the desk, showing them the makeshift holder she'd fashioned from a wastepaper basket.

Speaking in fluent, if Aussie-accented Japanese, she welcomed them and led them across to the desk. Were they all ill, or only one?

She pushed a form, printed in Japanese as well as English, across the desk, and the young man began to fill it in, at the same time explaining he was a tour guide and it was one of the women who was ill.

Rebecca introduced Stephanie, who led the sick young woman to a consulting room. As the area attracted predominantly Japanese tourists, all the staff in the clinic spoke at least a smattering of the language. Her own command of it was proficient, although medical terms defeated her.

Tonight, however, the tour guide, who'd followed the patient into the consulting room, could speak English, and it was he who explained that the holiday maker had a sore throat.

Stephanie began her examination by taking the young woman's pulse, feeling the fast beat and heated skin immediately. Explaining each move in Japanese while she worked, she then took her blood pressure—higher than it should have been for a young woman—and finally examined her throat.

The tonsils and pharynx were an angry red, with whitish blotches on the tonsils.

'We call it in English a strep throat,' Stephanie explained. 'A streptococcal infection. I can give you an injection of penicillin to start fighting it, then follow up with tablets to take. Have you had penicillin before?'

The young woman nodded.

'Did you have any allergic reaction?'

A definitive shake of her head.

'Have you any other allergies you know of?'

Again the head shake.

Stephanie rang for Joanne, the nurse on night duty, and, when she came, told her what she needed. As Joanne departed, Stephanie turned her attention back to her patient, concerned that the young woman, who was now shaking with feverish chills, would have to go back out into the inclement weather.

And possibly continue a gruelling 'holiday' schedule.

'Where are you staying?' she asked.

'Just down the road at the Whale Beach Resort,' the guide replied.

It *was* just down the road—perhaps only five hundred metres—but in the rain...

'I think you should get a taxi back there,' she told the man, speaking Japanese so the patient would also understand. 'And—' She checked the completed patient form '...Reiki should spend at least tomorrow in bed.'

'But tomorrow we go to see the dolphins!' It was Reiki who protested, and Stephanie knew it was useless to argue. The young woman had probably been feeling sick for days, but was soldiering on because she'd paid good money for her holiday and wanted to make the most of it.

However, the doctor in Stephanie had to make the effort.

'You should stay in bed,' she repeated. 'If you don't, you could become even sicker.'

Reiki's obsidian-dark eyes filled with tears, as if the thought of feeling worse was truly horrifying.

Maybe she'd listen to the advice.

Joanne returned and, after asking the guide to leave the room, Stephanie gave the intra-muscular injection of benzathine penicillin G into Reiki's buttock.

'Stay in bed,' she warned again, as she showed the young woman out.

'Bet she doesn't,' Rebecca said, when the three had departed.

But more patients had drifted in so, although Stephanie agreed, she didn't have time to chat.

Jet lag struck at midnight, but for a couple of hours Harry refused to give in to it.

'Damn it all, I took my melatonin, I was flying west to east. This isn't supposed to happen!'

He was striding back and forth in front of the wide windows of the apartment so kindly loaned to him by Bob Quayle. Outside, the rain still lashed down, blurring the streetlights and hiding from view the ocean he knew was only a block from where he stood.

'Maybe it doesn't happen when you're flying east-west, not west-east!' he muttered as he made his way to the kitchen and opened the refrigerator door, bending over to eye the edibles Pete Jennings, Bob's business manager, had organised for him.

No, it wasn't food he needed, but sleep.

He strode back to the living room and slumped into an armchair, wondering if it might be more conducive to sleep than the bed.

But nothing worked, except his brain, which was alive and alert and looking for some action.

Action!

Ha! Maybe that was the answer.

In return for the largesse of the apartment, he'd told Bob he'd take a look at the twenty-four-hour clinic somewhere downstairs in this very building. Twenty-four hours meant open all the time. It should be open and operating right now.

He leapt out of the chair, strode through to the bedroom, pulled on trousers and a long-sleeved shirt that could have done with an iron, but at two in the morning he didn't care, and headed down to ground level to find the ailing medical centre.

Steph was battling with Tom Butler, a regular patient with a bipolar condition. She'd seen Tom a few times when he was in his depressive phase of the illness—feeling suicidal and needing someone to assure him he was wanted on the earth—but tonight he was the opposite, flying high, not on drugs but on the curious chemical imbalance in his system that caused his mood swings.

'So I thought I'd come and show you how well I am,' he said, grabbing Steph and swinging her off the ground, then dancing around the waiting room with her in his arms.

'Put me down!' she shrieked, while Rebecca pressed the hidden alarm bell to summon a security man—just in case.

Steph heard the asthmatic wheeze the doors made as they opened, and tried to see if help—in the form of the security man—had arrived, but it wasn't until Tom completed his arc that she saw the newcomer. Tall and angular, his midnight-dark hair tousled and untidy, his so-familiar face a study in disbelief.

'Harry?'

Harry heard his name, and stared in total bewilderment at the woman dangling in the arms of a dancing maniac. The beautiful dark red hair was cut so close to her head she might have been shorn, while her face was too thin—all flat planes and angles and huge, huge eyes—but it was still Steph.

'Steph?'

He heard his voice say her name—heard the incredulous shock in it.

'Put me down!' she was saying to the man who held her. 'Now, Tom!'

The man not only ignored her but whirled her around once again, while, behind Harry, the doors slid open again and a very large security guard entered.

'Put me down, Tom,' Steph repeated, more sternly this time.

The dancing man—Tom—did just that, dropping his burden so Steph crashed to the floor. Instinct sent Harry towards her, rushing to her aid, his hand outstretched to help her to her feet.

She looked up at him, and flinched—the movement so apparent he drew back, muscles stiffening with shock, his heart wincing, his mind numb with regret.

Then she scrambled to her feet, thrust her hands on her hips and glared at him.

'If you're not here as a patient then get out right now,

Harry Pritchard,' she said, but her voice was shaking and her smoky grey eyes were bright with unshed tears.

Harry felt the wince become a clenching kind of pain. He opened his mouth to explain, but she'd moved away, motioning to the man who'd dropped her, sending him ahead of her into what was probably a consulting room.

'Are you a patient?'

For the first time he noticed another woman, this one behind a desk in the far corner of the waiting room, her arms folded as she awaited an answer from him.

'No, I'm to be working here,' he said, turning towards the security man to include him in the conversation. 'My name's Harry Pritchard. The new owner has asked me to take a look at the way things are run. His business manager was supposed to let you know.'

The woman behind the desk—Rebecca Harris if the name plaque was correct—studied him for a moment.

'We heard a bloke was coming,' she said, shrugging as if his arrival was a matter of supreme indifference to her. 'But we hardly expected you to start work in the early hours of the morning.'

'That was obvious!' Harry snapped, as a vivid picture of Steph in the man's arms flashed across his mind. 'Do those kind of shenanigans go on all the time? Do you all mix business with pleasure?'

Rebecca—if she was Rebecca, introductions had been bypassed—looked at him as if he was mad.

'Mix business with pleasure?' she repeated. She shook her head. 'I have no idea what you're talking about.'

'I'm talking about that man dancing around the waiting room with that woman in his arms,' Harry said, growing angrier—mainly with Steph—by the moment.

'But she didn't want to be in his arms,' Rebecca told him, still frowning dubiously at him. 'That's Tom. He's a patient. Bipolar, and apparently in a manic phase. Dr Prince came out to call him—he was the next patient—and he grabbed her. I called Security—that's what Ned's doing here.'

She nodded towards the large man who was still standing like a misplaced monolith just inside the front door.

'Oh!' Harry said, then struggled to find something else to add. 'I'm actually jet-lagged. I woke up and couldn't get back to sleep.'

They weren't the best couple of sentences to have found—pertaining as they did to a much earlier bit of the conversation. But as the woman showed no signs of rescuing him from this conversational morass, he plunged valiantly on.

'That's why I'm here at this hour.'

'You can go, Ned,' she said, looking past him to the security man, who touched his uniform cap and departed. 'As for you…' She turned back to Harry. 'I don't know what you're supposed to be doing, but I'd advise you to do it during the daytime in future. From the sound of things, you know Dr Prince, and if she's not happy having you here when she's on duty, then neither am I.'

Harry watched her draw herself up to her full five feet six and puff out her chest as birds did when they wanted to make themselves look bigger, and fiercer—and he had to smile.

'Actually,' he said, hoping his voice sounded properly apologetic, 'Dr Prince has no say over when I'm here and when I'm not. But I will try not to antagonise her.'

Lie! Of course he'd antagonise her. He didn't even have to try. There was so much unfinished business between them it was inevitable.

CHAPTER TWO

SOMEHOW, Stephanie managed to calm Tom down enough for him to answer questions about his medication.

'But I don't need it when I'm well,' he told her. She forced herself to concentrate on the patient, explaining slowly and carefully that it was just as important when he was feeling well as when he was depressed.

'It keeps the chemicals in your body balanced,' she told him—for possibly the twentieth time since he'd first become her patient.

'But I'm better now,' he argued, though in the end he agreed to take the tablets—but only because she'd asked him to.

The phone buzzed, and she turned to Tom.

'Rebecca only interrupts if it's something urgent,' she said to him, hoping he'd take the hint.

But, being Tom, he didn't.

'I'm as urgent as anyone,' he said, his jaw setting belligerently.

'Of course you are—and more important because you're a regular—but this could be a child in serious trouble, Tom. I have to go.'

She stood up and walked towards the door, praying he'd follow because there was no way she could leave him in a consulting room on his own.

He did follow, but as he reached the door he grabbed her again.

'Ah, my favourite doctor,' he cried, lifting her from

behind this time so she was able to kick back with her heel, hitting him in the knee.

Bang. Down she went again, while Tom clutched his knee and scowled.

'You didn't have to do that!' he grumbled at her, but as he turned, as if to touch her again, Harry appeared, seizing Tom by the elbow and steering him towards the reception desk.

'There's a woman in the second consulting room, coughing badly and slightly cyanotic around the lips.'

Joanne had appeared and now helped Steph to her feet, then drew her towards the second door.

'I've put an oxygen mask on her.'

She thrust a new patient form into Stephanie's hand, then opened the door and followed Steph into the room.

The woman was sitting on the examination couch, clutching the oxygen mask in one hand while she coughed and wheezed and gasped for breath. Steph could smell the mix of cigarette smoke and alcohol fumes from the door, but to give the woman her due, she might not have been smoking. A person's hair and clothing could absorb the smell just being in some of the nightclubs where smoking was still allowed.

'Put the mask back over your nose and mouth and breathe deeply,' she said when the spasm of coughing stopped. 'And don't try to answer—just nod or shake your head.'

The woman nodded to indicated she understood.

'I'm going to listen to your chest. Have you had this kind of attack before?'

Another nod.

'Has it been diagnosed?'

Again the agreement.

'Bronchitis?'

Nod.

'Chronic?'

Nod.

'Do you use a puffer of any kind?'

The woman shook her head.

'Take any preventative drugs regularly?'

Another head shake.

Stephanie finished her examination and straightened up, looking directly into the eyes of the woman who was now breathing more easily.

'Do you smoke?'

The woman nodded, and her eyes shifted, suggesting she'd been told—probably more than once—she should give it up for the sake of her health.

'And it's worth it even though you have to put up with attacks like this?' Steph asked.

The woman shook her head.

'I'll give you antibiotics now to help you through this attack, but the problem is,' Steph continued, 'if you keep on having these crises it will eventually affect your heart. I can't see any sign of it yet, but there's a condition called cor pulmonale where, because of the extra work it's called on to do, the section of the heart that deals with blood flow to your lungs becomes enlarged. This is serious stuff, so it's up to you to decide if you want to risk it.'

She waited a moment for this to sink in.

'Your own GP has probably told you all the things you need to do to get rid of the bronchitis, but I'll repeat them. First is give up smoking—there are really good medications available to help with that these days. Then you need to increase your exercise—walking is the best, starting slowly then building up until you're comfortable walking briskly for at least twenty minutes every day.'

She went on to ask the woman about allergies, and prescribed ampicillin and a bronchodilator, which would help prevent bad attacks if used when wheezing first started.

'But it's mainly a matter of avoiding irritants until your lungs are in better shape,' she added. 'As well as cigarette smoke, things like hair spray, aerosol insect sprays, even occupational chemicals can all affect damaged lungs.'

The woman—Beth Graham, Steph had finally deciphered the writing on the patient form—now removed the mask.

'That's all very easy for you to say,' Beth snapped, 'but it's impossible to do. I'm a barmaid. I work in cigarette smoke all the time—and I've tried all the patches and tablets ever invented in an effort to stop smoking. Then I think, Why bother when I have to breathe in other people's smoke in my job? As for chemical irritants, you should smell the stuff we use to clean out the beer pipes and the area behind the bar when we close up for the night. I love doctors who say do this and do that, and never think about whether it's possible or not.'

'I'm sorry,' Steph said. 'We do tend to preach.'

She studied Beth's tired face, then checked the form again. At thirty-five, Beth was only five years older than Steph herself.

'There's no other job? Or maybe a day shift so you're not out in the night air—and don't have to do the cleaning?'

Beth shook her head.

'I've three kids—the oldest is fifteen, so I can leave her in charge at night, but the baby's only six and I want to be home for her when she goes to school and comes home. Earlier shifts just don't work.'

Steph raised her hands out from her sides.

'Tell me about it!' she said. 'I'm not exactly crazy about working nights myself, but I've a four-year-old and I feel the same way about being home for her.'

They talked a little longer, Steph trying to think of alternative occupations for a woman who preferred to work at night.

'I've tried a few others,' Beth said. 'Drove a limo for a while, but nothing pays as well as night-shift bar work and with Desiree, my eldest, now wanting all the things teenagers want, I need the money.'

'But it shouldn't be at the expense of your health,' Stephanie said. 'Have you considered retraining? Doing a course that might get you into something you can do at home?'

Beth nodded, then shrugged.

'And who keeps us while I do the course? That's what it always comes back to, doesn't it?'

She picked up the scripts and Steph walked with her to the door, then, as Beth departed, Steph continued on to the reception desk.

'We could form a club of women who work nights so they can be home for their kids during the day. That was another one.'

'Well, I'm only doing it for another year at the most,' Rebecca said. 'Once Dyson's in high school, I reckon it's going to be more important for me to be home nights than days. It'll mean a pay cut, but you just wait—I'm going to get a receptionist job in a real doctors' surgery, where you get to know the patients and have regulars bringing in bottles of jam and crocheted facecloths.'

Stephanie laughed.

'We have our regulars,' she reminded Rebecca. 'Look at Tom!'

'And a couple of drunken derelicts, and a group of homeless kids,' Rebecca snorted. 'Some regulars!'

Harry, sitting in the administrator's office flicking through files in a drawer on the left hand side of the desk, heard them talking. The administrator's office must have been an afterthought, built by putting a thin partition across part of the reception area, so the sound carried easily.

The conversation was revealing enough in its way, but in other ways he was more confused than ever.

Seeing Steph again was the primary source of confusion, but beyond that so many things didn't even begin to add up, he wasn't sure where to start sorting them out.

Did Bob Quayle know Steph was working at the clinic—and, if so, why hadn't he mentioned it?

And why was Steph talking as if she *had* to work, and juggle work and child-care? Even if Martin had left no money when he'd died, surely the Quayles could afford to provide financial support for their only grandchild?

The two women were still talking—about children now. Rebecca was complaining about the language kids picked up at school.

'You know the bloke I said was coming in?' she added, switching conversation with the rapidity only a woman could manage. 'Well, that's him—the chap you know. The one you called Harry. He's the bloke Muriel mentioned in her note.'

Harry tried to imagine Steph's reaction and failed, but now they were talking about him, he'd better make his continued presence known, in case they didn't realise how thin the wall between them was.

'Harry's the bloke?' he heard Steph say as he rose from behind the desk. 'What do you mean?'

'He's here to see how the clinic runs.' Rebecca expanded on her explanation.

'At three in the morning? You've got to be kidding!'

'Jet lag!' Rebecca explained, as Harry opened the door and stepped out.

'Good morning, Steph,' he said, hoping he sounded more confident than he felt. 'How's everything with you?'

She gave him a look that would have made a lesser man turn tail and run, but he'd been on the receiving end of Steph's black looks before, and was able to ignore it. But he couldn't ignore the alarm he felt, seeing her so pale and tired looking, and far too thin—yet, strangely, more beautiful than she'd ever been.

'What, exactly, are you doing here?' she demanded, ignoring his question and going on the attack instead.

'Checking out the place for the new owner.' Now Bob Quayle's request to keep his identity a secret seemed odder than ever. But wouldn't Steph know her father-in-law was the new owner? 'Apparently the clinic was in financial difficulties when the current owners bought it and the directors of the company would like to know why.' Damn the woman—he was becoming more and more confused.

Her eyes narrowed with suspicion.

'Oh, yes! I can just see the headlines!' she sniped. '"Eminent cosmetic surgeon takes on investigation into dead-broke, run-down medical centre".' She used her long slim fingers to provide the quotation marks. 'You've certainly got the qualifications! Not!'

'It's a favour for a friend,' Harry said, remaining calm though the urge to shake her was becoming stronger by the second. 'And you know I've worked in places like this before.'

He was explaining too much, he realised, so he added a curt, 'Not that it's any of your business,' just to put her in her place.

But Steph had never known her place—which, in days gone by, Harry had felt had been in his bed rather than Martin's—and she stepped towards him, suspicion now radiating from her in almost visible waves.

'What friend?' she demanded, but before he could reply—or duck a reply—the doors opened again and three obviously inebriated youths came in, two of them supporting the third who was bleeding profusely from a head wound.

'He fell over,' one explained, as the threesome lurched and staggered closer to the desk.

Steph responded first, stepping forward and taking hold of the injured man, telling Rebecca to get details and call Joanne to the treatment room.

The first thing I tell Bob Quayle, Harry thought as he swept around the desk in time to support the other side of the injured youth, is that women shouldn't be working night shifts in a place like this.

'It's ridiculous!' he growled, only realising he'd spoken aloud when Steph turned and raised an eyebrow in his direction.

'There being only women here.' He put his thoughts into words, while he steered their patient towards a table set up in the middle of the room. 'Look at you—so thin a decent puff of wind would blow you over! How are you expected to manage drunks like this?'

The youth had lurched across the table and was going a peculiar green shade, but Steph had clearly been here before because she grabbed a basin and held it while the youngster threw up a great deal of the evening's alcohol intake.

The nurse, slightly better built than Steph but still no Amazon, now appeared and bustled about, emptying the dish, cleaning up the man's face with a towel, producing a tray with antiseptic solution on it so Steph, who now had her patient sitting on the table, could clean the head wound.

Fuming inwardly at the absurdity of the situation, Harry remained on the far side, one hand resting on the patient's arm in case restraint was necessary.

Steph was talking, asking the lad his name—Jerry—and what they'd been celebrating to be out so late on a week-night.

Jerry launched into a somewhat disjointed explanation that was still logical enough to assure Harry—and no doubt Steph as well—that he wasn't suffering concussion as a result of the head wound.

'How did it happen, do you remember?' Steph asked.

'Fell off the railing,' Jerry told her.

'Railing?'

Jerry grinned.

'The one around the fountain in the mall. We were going to take a swim and Todd said first we'd better walk around the railing to see if we were sober enough.'

'Of course,' Steph said, as if such outrageous behaviour was perfectly logical to her. Then she glanced at Harry and grinned. 'It's a good test but not everyone passes it.'

And Harry remembered.

They'd been in first year Med—or maybe it had been second—a long time ago anyway. Holidaying at Martin's family home after the exams, celebrating the end of semester, and Martin saying they had to walk around the railing to prove sobriety before they could swim in the fountain.

Steph had been the only one who'd made it all the way round…

Steph, with her long, lean limbs and lissom grace…

She was suturing the cut and talking soothingly to Jerry as she stitched, establishing he was a local, not a tourist, explaining he should see his own GP in a week to have the stitches removed.

'I'd rather come here for you to do it,' Jerry said, making a grab for Steph's hand.

'I know you would,' she agreed pleasantly, while eas-ily avoiding his grasping hand. 'But I might not be on duty and you'd get a big, rough, bearded first-year doctor who'd rip them out without caring whether it hurts or not. Best go to your own GP.'

She cut a waterproof dressing and put it over the top.

'Don't take that off,' she warned, then she helped him off the table.

He went pale again, and the nurse produced the basin, but the lad steadied, and even had the grace to apologise for throwing up earlier.

'That's OK,' Steph told him. 'But you go straight home now.'

He nodded, felt the injured place on his head with careful fingers, then let Steph lead him to the door. Though Harry wanted to follow, he restrained himself and instead introduced himself to the nurse.

'Are you always on night duty?' he asked, conscious of the fact he was supposed to be doing a job.

Joanne shook her head.

'Twice a week,' she explained. 'That's all I need to do because the pay is higher for night duty and I make as much on two nights as I would on three and a half day shifts. I'm a student and when it's not busy I study.

Steph's very good—she only calls me in if she needs something.'

I'm sure she does, Harry thought—thinking of everyone but herself.

He talked to Joanne for a while longer, discovering she was studying for a higher degree in nursing and hoping to go into teaching eventually.

'Teaching has better hours for when I have a family,' she explained, and Harry shook his head, seeing once again the problem of shuffling work and family.

He walked out of the treatment room, still thinking about it—though his thinking ability was declining as his jet-lag phase switched from full alert to heavy-eyed exhaustion.

He'd have to think about it later.

Think about Bob Quayle and the job later as well.

But not Steph—he'd talk to her now.

She was nowhere in sight, and behind the reception desk Rebecca was chatting to an alert-looking woman in a vivid red suit. She was of medium height, and very pretty, with sleek blonde hair pulled back into a neat pleat at the back of her head.

'This is Linda—she's the early-shift receptionist this week,' Rebecca said, waving him towards the desk. 'She'll introduce you to the other day staff. That's if you're still in hyperactive mode and want to stay.'

She turned to Linda.

'He's Harry Pritchard—working for the new owners—checking to see we all do our jobs and don't pinch money from the till.'

'Some hope of that,' Linda said, 'when most of our patients are on Medicare.'

But she smiled at Harry and gave him an assessing

look—then another, much warmer smile as she added, 'But if I can help you in any way, just let me know.'

Harry smiled politely and excused himself. She'd put too much emphasis on the 'any' for him to miss the meaning, but he wasn't interested in pretty blondes—not right now.

Right now—as the night shift had apparently ended— he wanted to catch a certain redhead before she left work, and demand answers to at least some of the questions jostling for attention in his head.

He'd explored the place earlier and found the tearoom, which appeared to double as a staff cloakroom, but though Joanne was there, chatting to a young man about the night they'd had, there was no sign of Steph.

'She's gone,' Rebecca told him, when he emerged and was looking down the corridor towards the back entrance to the clinic.

'I beg your pardon?' Harry snapped, sure he hadn't been so obvious in his quest.

'Steph! She's gone. She likes to get home before Fanny wakes up and her old car's so unreliable she shoots out the moment the relieving doctor arrives. That way, if it doesn't start, she can walk home and still be there for Fanny.'

Disappointment blurred with anger that she'd taken off without so much as a good-bye—but, then, she'd hardly been welcoming, had she?

Harry nodded curtly to Rebecca and strode back to the administration office. He'd flicked idly through the main bank of filing cabinets in the early hours of the morning, now he'd take a closer look. Personnel files would have employees' addresses. Though he'd always assumed she still lived with the Quayles—he'd been sending Fanny's presents to that address.

But if she lived with Bob and Doreen, then she'd know Bob owned the clinic. Wouldn't she?

Damn her, dashing off like that—he really needed to talk to her.

Forget it! common sense said. You're far too tired to think, let alone carry on a sensible conversation—especially with a woman who hates your guts.

But as he made his way back up to the apartment—Bob Quayle's apartment—his mind continued to question what he'd seen and heard and learnt.

Nothing made sense—least of all Bob Quayle asking him to check out the clinic.

And not mentioning Steph worked there...

Not mentioning Steph at all!

It was still raining—it already seemed like forty days and forty nights—as Steph drove home. The not unpleasant weariness she usually felt after a night on duty had deserted her and in its place a high-strung tension sang and shimmied along her nerves.

For a start, there was Harry.

No, Harry wasn't so much a start as a huge, gigantic, enormous and probably insurmountable obstacle the misaligned planets had dropped into her life. Like a meteorite so dense she could see no way through or around or over it.

A meteorite with a distinct whiff of fish.

She wasn't naïve enough to believe Harry had just happened into her workplace. Fate wasn't that cute.

And a cosmetic surgeon appointed to check the running of a twenty-four-hour clinic? The fish smell was becoming stronger.

She drove slowly through the deserted streets—not

even the most dedicated of joggers were out this morning—while her mind tossed up possible explanations.

Harry's second cousin's wife had bought the business and he was doing her a favour?

He was here for a quick visit and this filled in the time?

His parents had left their property in the west and retired to Summerland? Maybe *they* had bought the clinic as an investment, and he was checking it out for them? Ah, now that was feasible, wasn't it?

If you believed in fairy stories...

She pulled into her drive, thoughts of Harry set aside for a moment as she did the mental arithmetic she usually did on mornings like this. If she bought absolutely nothing but essentials for the next six months, she'd have enough money saved to build the garage she badly needed for the car—then, three months after that, enough for a covered walkway from the garage to the house.

Nine months—that wasn't long. Like being pregnant. That had passed.

Bad comparison.

She slumped forward in the seat and rested her head on the steering-wheel. She considered thumping it there once or twice to empty out the thoughts she didn't want to have, then, realising Fanny could be waking any minute, she straightened up, found her umbrella, eased open the car door and made the dash across her muddy back yard to the door.

Her house was warm, and silent in the comforting way that told her all within were sleeping soundly. She checked Fanny anyway, smiling to herself as she looked at the little body splayed across the bed, rosy cheeked from sleep, gold curls tousled around her small head.

Making her way back to the kitchen, Steph poked her

head around Tracy's door as well, flinching at the mess then remembering she'd been a messy teenager herself. There'd been so much to see, and do, and learn, there'd never been time to put things away.

Satisfied all was well in this, the most important corner of her small world, Steph put on the kettle, popped bread into the toaster and wondered how long it would be before her budget would stretch to a home-delivered daily paper.

'It would have been wet this morning, anyway,' she comforted herself, turning on the radio instead, so at least she'd learn something of what was happening in the world from the morning news.

Fanny erupted into the kitchen as Steph finished her toast.

'I forgot,' she told her mother, casting herself into Steph's arms for a good-morning kiss and hug. 'Today we have to take our favourite toy to kindy for a toys' teaparty.'

'Well, that's OK,' Steph said, smoothing hair back from her daughter's forehead. 'You've plenty to choose from.'

'But that's the problem,' Fanny said with a dramatic sigh.

Steph smiled to herself, knowing she used the same phrase to Tracy all the time—usually when discussing either their individual timetables or budgeting considerations.

'What's the problem?' she asked the little drama queen now snuggled on her lap.

'I don't know what's my favourite.'

Another huge sigh.

'You're taking Bear to bed these days, maybe you could take him.'

'But then Adeline will get cross,' Fanny told her.

Steph, knowing this conversation could go on for two days, opted out.

'Well, you run back to your bedroom and have a look at all of them while I fix your breakfast. You can get dressed while you're thinking and call me when you're ready for me to do your hair.'

Fanny accepted this suggestion with good grace, and in the end decided Bear should share the kindy treat.

Steph tied a red ribbon around his neck, finishing it with a big bow so he looked properly festive, then, with Fanny and the bear both wrapped in her raincoat, she carried the pair out to the car and drove down the road to the kindergarten.

'Don't forget Tracy's picking you up this afternoon,' she reminded her daughter.

'Because it's Friday!' Fanny said, showing off her knowledge of their routine.

Steph kissed her goodbye, checked that the kindergarten staff knew Tracy would collect Fanny, then departed. If she went straight home, she could get in five hours' straight sleep.

If she didn't let thoughts of Harry's unexpected re-emergence in her life intrude, she *might* get five hours' straight sleep.

But how could she not think about it…?

Not think about Harry with his dark, all-seeing eyes, and his long, lanky bushman's body…

She must have slept eventually, for she woke at one, unrefreshed—in fact, so fuzzy and disoriented she knew she needed a whole lot more.

She could doze for another hour, or do a quick house-clean and wash. With the wet weather, everything felt damp.

Opting for housework, she clambered out of bed, made herself a cup of tea and a sandwich, then put on a wash and whipped through the housework. When she had a garage she could hang washing in it when it rained, she reminded herself as she spread the wet clothes over drying frames on the front veranda.

Or maybe, after the garage but before the covered walkway, she could buy a dryer.

'Dream on, Prince!' she muttered to herself, late now and needing to hurry to get to the local medical centre by three.

Fifteen women, in various stages of pregnancy, greeted her enthusiastically. Although the public hospital offered antenatal classes for pregnant women, it was a long way to travel for a half-hour session, so Steph, in conjunction with a local medical practice, did an hour a week, combining their regular health checks with information on nutrition and the process of childbirth, followed by breathing and exercise classes. It was a nice little supplement to her income and she enjoyed the interaction with the women, sharing their excitement as they approached the birth.

But this afternoon the usual joy was missing, and she made her way home afterwards, eager to see Fanny, but unable to blot from her mind thoughts of Harry Pritchard and his sudden reappearance in her life.

'Forget him,' she told herself, as she swung into the drive, nearly hitting the car already parked there.

She frowned at the intruder, a dark green sedan, its shape suggesting it was a fairly recent model.

Had one of the kindy mothers given Tracy and Fanny a lift home, and been invited in for coffee?

Or perhaps someone had driven Tracy home from lectures then stayed on so she could collect Fanny in a car, rather than walking her home through the rain.

Steph considered these and other options, then wondered why she didn't just get out of her car and go inside—find out who the stranger was.

Because it meant dashing through the rain and she was sick and tired of being wet.

And if whoever owned the car wanted to leave before her—which was likely as she didn't leave until after eight—she'd have to dash out again and shift her car.

With grudging reluctance, she started her car again, backed out and parked beside the kerb opposite her front gate. Slightly further to dash, but what the hell. Being wet was minor compared to other problems she had right now.

One of which was sitting on her front veranda, almost hidden among the drying racks and draped laundry.

'What are you doing here?' Steph demanded, staring in disbelief at the man who'd sabotaged her thoughts, ruined her sleep and had now invaded her home.

'Your babysitter told me she wasn't allowed to invite strangers in without your permission,' he said, rising to his feet so he towered over her in the limited space left by the washing. 'And though Fanny acknowledged she had an Uncle Harry, she produced so ancient a photo of me, no one could see the resemblance.'

He gave a small, apologetic smile—an expression so familiar Steph felt her heart cramp with pain.

'We compromised by me staying on the veranda—because of the rain—until you came home and introduced us.'

Another smile—another cramp.

'Fanny does seem quite anxious to meet me,' he said, sliding in under her defences.

Steph stared at him in disbelief.

'Why are you doing this? Why are you here? What's going on, Harry?'

Her voice was so full of pain and anxiety, Harry found himself wincing again. What had happened to make her so tense and suspicious?

OK, so they hadn't parted friends—in fact, she'd vowed to never speak to him again—but she'd always sent thank-you notes for the gifts he'd sent to Fanny, and Steph had never been one to hold a grudge.

He shook his head, realising he had no idea how to answer her—and no inkling of the answers to his own mental queries.

Fanny broke the deadlock. The beautiful child, with eyes so like Martin's Harry found himself staring at her, appeared in the doorway, the old photo still held in one hand.

'This man says he's Uncle Harry!' she said to her mother, casting a stern look in Harry's direction as she spoke.

Harry saw Steph hesitate. He'd heard enough of Fanny's conversation with the babysitter to know Steph had spoken kindly of him to her little daughter. Now she was stuck in a dilemma of her own making—did she throw him out then explain to Fanny why she'd lost her godfather, or invite him in and pretend he was the friend Fanny thought him?

'He is Uncle Harry,' Steph said, kneeling beside the little girl and giving her a kiss and a quick hug. 'He's just got older so he doesn't look quite the same as he does in your photo, but if you look at his eyes in the photo and then at his real eyes, you'll see they're the same. And his smile…'

She looked up at Harry, her own eyes as cool as ice water.

'Smile, Uncle Harry,' she ordered—voice even cooler than the eyes. 'See,' she added, turning back to Fanny. 'It's kind of like the same smile.'

It was nothing like the same smile, and Harry knew it. He knew the photo Fanny held for comparison, because he had an identical one himself. It had been taken when he'd first realised he loved Steph—loved her as more than a friend—and that love had shone in the smile.

Even though she hadn't seen it.

CHAPTER THREE

Once assured this was her Uncle Harry in the flesh, Fanny took over, inviting him in, taking him into her room to become reacquainted with all the toys he'd sent her over the years, chattering on as if she'd known him for ever.

Which, in a way, she had, Steph realised.

Tracy, too, was obviously impressed by the visitor, apologising for her earlier doubts, offering tea or coffee. If Steph hadn't been so disturbed by his presence in her house, she'd have laughed at the way the pair of them vied for his attention.

It was almost inevitable that Fanny would invite him to stay for dinner, Steph realised later as she added a tin of tomatoes to the mince she was making up into shepherd's pie for their meal.

Though not as inevitable that he'd say yes!

What was he doing here?

Why had Harry come back?

She sneaked looks at him when she thought he was well occupied with Fanny's chatter—saw the slight lines nearly five years had left in his face. Caught glimpses of his brown eyes, glowing with good humour and kindness as he talked to her daughter.

Did he feel a bond with Fanny because he'd seen her born—because he'd held Steph's hand right through the delivery? Taken Martin's place because Martin—no, she wasn't going to follow that particular strand of memory…

Somehow she got through the meal, but when Harry offered to wash up, she knew she couldn't share the kitchen with him a minute longer.

'Good,' she said. 'Tracy and Fanny can help you and I'll have my shower. I wouldn't mind getting to work early tonight, I've some paperwork to do.'

She whipped away, showered, then, wrapped in a towel, dashed across the hall to her bedroom. Where she surveyed the contents of her wardrobe and sighed.

Jeans and a T-shirt. It's what you always wear to work, she reminded herself, but tonight she wished she had a new T-shirt or one pair of slightly less faded jeans. Tonight she'd have liked to look—well, attractive…

For Harry?

Or because he's a man?

She tried to tell herself it was because he was a man and it was normal for the female of the species to preen for men, but she didn't believe it for a moment. She wanted to look good for Harry, because Harry had always told her she was beautiful.

Though usually the assurances had come when she'd broken up with a boyfriend and had been in need of a confidence boost! Back in the early years of their friendship, they'd shared the highs and lows of their relationships with the opposite sex. Harry and Martin vetting the boys she went out with; she introducing them to girls she knew, giving them advice—from her admittedly limited experience—on how to win a woman…

She peered dolefully into the mirror.

Beautiful?

Bah! As if it matters what you look like, or what Harry used to tell you. What should be occupying your mind is what he's doing here, and whether whatever it is will impact on the hard-won security of your little family.

She pulled on her oldest pair of jeans and a T-shirt that had a mouse with boxing gloves shaping up to an elephant—a gift from Tracy—then sallied forth, ready to do battle to protect her home and daughter from whatever new threat might be hovering above their heads.

'Love the shirt!' Harry said, when his eyes had raked over her and showed more disapproval than admiration.

'Whatever I wear is covered by a coat anyway,' she told him, shrugging off his reactions and turning her attention to Fanny.

'Bedtime for you, kid,' she said, but the excitement of meeting Uncle Harry in the flesh had gone to Fanny's head and, in a rare display of contrariness, she argued.

'What if I read you a story when you're in bed?' Harry offered, and, as Fanny's tantrum turned to smiles, Steph felt her insides knot with a mix of anger and something that could only be jealousy.

Determined not to let it show, she forced a smile, then took Fanny's hand and led her off.

But hiding her emotions only made things worse, for they seethed and bubbled inside her, so when it was finally time to leave for work, she was so uptight she flooded the car engine and then couldn't get the wretched vehicle started.

The passenger door opened and Harry poked his head in.

'Come on, I'll drive you,' he said.

'Don't bother, I can get a cab!' she snapped.

'You're still as stubborn as a mule, Stephanie Prince!' Harry said. 'But you were never stupid. How easy do you think it will be to get a cab in this weather on a Friday night? Besides, we need to talk.'

'No, we don't,' Steph told him, but he was right about the cab situation. Cursing under her breath, she gathered up her handbag and found her umbrella, then clambered out into the rain.

Again!

'Nice car!' she muttered as she strapped her damp body into the passenger seat, and sniffed the newness appreciatively.

'It's a hire car. I've only been back a week—less, really.'

She glanced across at him, backing expertly out of her drive, and wondered at how things had gone so wrong that she and Harry were reduced to such an inane conversation.

'What are you doing here?' she asked again—though this time she was going to get an answer.

He turned and grinned at her and she felt a tide of emotion swamp over her, so deep and forceful she must surely drown.

'In the car?' he teased. 'Driving you to work. In Summerland? I've come to work here—to open a specialist clinic.'

'Well, you've come to the right place,' Steph retorted, upset because the thought of Harry being permanently in the place she now called home had thrown her into more turmoil. 'Plenty of wealthy, aging women wanting to look younger.'

The glance Harry cast her way this time had no amusement in it at all.

'You used not to be bitchy, Steph,' he said in a voice cooler than the rain beyond the windows. 'It was one of the things that made you special.'

'Special enough to be Martin's wife, but only one of his many women,' she snapped. 'Well, that Stephanie's gone, Harry. I've had enough bad things happen to me lately to justify me being the bitchiest woman in the world for the rest of my life.'

Harry tried to speak, but the thought of what Steph must have gone through stopped his breath. And she'd said 'lately'. Bad things were still happening? Or had happened recently?

Since the terrible night when she'd given birth to Fanny, and Martin had been killed, racing to get to the hospital? Late because no one had been able to contact him. Late because he'd been away, not at the conference he'd used as an excuse but on a stolen weekend with another woman…

'OK,' he said at last, 'I guess that's up to you.'

Harry glanced at her again, but she was staring out the window, studying the rain as if someone might later question her about its force or wetness. But the shape of her head, visible beneath the short-cropped hair, was beautiful, and he had to grip the steering-wheel more tightly to stop his hand reaching out and his fingers feeling those newly revealed bones.

'You can drop me in front of the clinic,' she said, turning away from the window, but only to stare out through the windscreen—determined not to look at him.

'No, I'll take you through into the car park,' he said. 'I need to park the car. I'm coming to work with you.'

That got her! Steph's head swivelled so fast it was a wonder she didn't rick her neck.

'You're what?'

'Coming to work with you,' he repeated, and made no effort not to sound smug. 'Friday night—two doctors on duty. I've been asked to see how the place runs, so how better to achieve that than by working there?'

'You can't do this to me!' she stormed, her hands

curled into such tight fists he knew it was only with difficulty she refrained from pummelling him.

He pulled into one of the doctors' spaces behind the clinic and turned to her.

'Do what, Steph?' he asked quietly.

'Come back into my life like this. Haunt me this way. Why, Harry? Why?'

She was so distressed he reached out and rested the back of his fingers, oh, so lightly against her cheek.

'I would never do anything to hurt you, Steph, you must know that. And as for haunting you—I didn't know you were working in the clinic. Yes, I'd have contacted you, probably tomorrow or the next day. I wanted to see Fanny. Wanted to see you…'

There—he'd said it. But whatever reaction he'd expected it certainly wasn't to hear Steph laugh.

True, there was an edge of hysteria to the laughter, but she was still laughing.

'I don't believe it,' she said, shaking her head, then turning to him so he saw the wetness of tears glistening on her sculpted cheek-bones. 'First, however many years ago it was, fate put us together because of our surnames. Now you're telling me it brought you here—in a city of thirty thousand people—to the very place I work?'

He wasn't sure from her tone whether she was pleased or displeased with the machinations of fate, but Harry suspected it wasn't fate at all, but Bob Quayle who'd brought them back together. And the suspicion rested uneasily on his shoulders.

Once before, he'd kept a secret from Steph—the secret of Martin's continual and continuing infidelity—and it had cost him her friendship. Now he had another secret to keep. Martin's father's secret.

Steph opened the car door and stepped out. She knew

Harry must think she was mad, but the tension inside her had been winding tighter and tighter, and when he'd said he'd wanted to see her, something had ripped open.

Harry had wanted to see her...

If he only knew how often she'd felt the same way—how often she'd longed to see him, talk to him, feel the security of his friendship.

His love...

She walked into the clinic, knowing he was following, so aware of him her entire back prickled as if she'd come out in a rash.

And things only got worse.

Friday night began, as it usually did, quietly enough, but at about ten-thirty a woman came in, accompanied by her husband and another couple with whom they'd been at dinner. All four had enjoyed pre-dinner drinks, wine with dinner and a liqueur to finish the evening. While not boisterously intoxicated, they were still relaxed enough to be uninhibitedly noisy.

'It just happened,' the husband said, pointing to his wife's face. 'We all saw it kind of drooping and now she can't feel anything.'

The others joined in with descriptions of the woman's problem, while the actual patient looked far from worried, blaming it on the red wine which she normally didn't drink.

With difficulty, Steph detached her from the group and took her into a consulting room.

'I'm just going to touch you in various places to see what feeling you've got,' she told the woman, using first her fingers, then the end of a pair of sharp forceps to find the extent of the loss of feeling in the woman's face.

'It looks like Bell's palsy, a paralysis of the facial nerve.' She unrolled a chart on the wall, and pointed to the nerve. 'It can be caused by injury of some kind, or an infection, or maybe compression of the nerve inside the brain.'

'Like a tumour?'

'It's a possibility that you'll have to rule out,' Steph told her, 'but quite often it just happens and we put it down to some infection you were probably unaware of having.'

'Will it go away?' the woman asked, pressing desperate fingers to the numb side of her face.

'It might,' Steph told her. 'It's hard to predict. It can be transient or permanent, it can affect both sides of the face or, as in your case, only one. The main problem is with your eye.'

She held up a small mirror so the woman could see the obvious droop of one side of her mouth and one eyelid.

'Try blinking,' she suggested, and was relieved when the eyelid moved, if only slightly.

'Blinking spreads a sheet of moisture across your eyes, protecting them from drying out. I'll give you some liquid that simulates tears, and I want you to use it regularly—at least until you've seen your own GP and made arrangements to see a specialist to have possible causes ruled out.'

'But what about my mouth—and my eyelid? What if it doesn't go away? I don't want it to stay that way.'

'I know there are surgical procedures that can help,' she said, then realised she had someone on the spot who could explain these far better than she could. She lifted her phone and spoke to Rebecca, who put her through to Harry.

'My patient is just leaving,' he said, when Steph explained, briefly, what she wanted. 'I'll pop in as soon as

I've seen him out.' He was as good as his word, appearing within minutes, then examining the woman's face and explaining what could be done should the condition prove permanent.

'So it wouldn't be noticeable at all?' she asked, and Steph saw the slight puckering of a frown as Harry considered his reply.

It was a silly thing to go all limp-boned about, but it was so familiar—so Harry somehow—worrying how to say something so it caused the least pain.

'We can't work miracles,' he told the woman, 'and if the condition is permanent we can't make the muscles work again, but there is a lot we can do, cosmetically, to fix the slackness.'

He smiled encouragingly and the woman nodded. And though Harry hadn't given her any really good news, she seemed a lot happier.

Amazing what a smile will do, Steph thought, especially one of Harry's smiles.

The thought pulled her up—maybe she *had* become bitchy!

Harry departed and she walked the patient out, realising, as she saw the waiting room, that the usual Friday night mayhem was developing nicely. If Harry Pritchard wanted some action, he'd certainly get some tonight.

By two, the rush had died down. Two teenage girls who'd become ill drinking cocktails had been packed into a cab and sent home; three youths who'd been kicked out of a nightclub then started a fight with a twenty-stone bouncer had been despatched to A and E at the general hospital for X-rays; and a woman who had a child with croup had been comforted with cups of tea while a humidifier had eased the little boy's terrible barking cough.

With a temporary lull in the patient flow, Steph headed for the tearoom. When she'd first begun work at the clinic, a refrigerator in the room had been stocked with packets of sandwiches, and the staff had been free to help themselves to a snack. But these days—she guessed since the new owner took over—the sandwiches had disappeared and she usually brought her own snack.

But tonight, with Harry in the house, she'd forgotten.

She was searching through the cupboards, hoping to find a leftover biscuit, when the delicious smell of fresh coffee alerted her to another presence in the room.

'Ready for a snack?'

Harry was standing just inside the doorway, a box with four coffees held in one hand and a white plastic bag dangling from his fingers.

'I spent long enough in the US to learn the benefits of doughnuts as a quick carbohydrate boost,' he said, setting the coffee on the table and opening the plastic bag to reveal a box of garishly decorated doughnuts.

He must have seen Steph's dubious look, for he added, 'Actually, it was the only place open in this complex that sold both coffee and food. I figured the closer I was to the clinic the hotter the coffee would be. Help yourself—I'll take two cups out to reception. Rebecca and tonight's nurse—Peter, I think is his name—are playing some on-going card game.'

Steph selected one of the remaining cups of coffee, added a couple of straws of sugar which Harry had brought along and stirred it, then studied the doughnuts he'd left behind.

The least lurid was one with jam and cream so she picked it up, eased a little of the filling into the bin, then bit in.

It was absolutely delicious, the sweetness flooding her mouth.

'Ooh!' She all but whimpered out her delight, then looked at the remaining bite of the doughnut.

It couldn't possibly have been that good. She must have been starving to have even considered eating it. She popped the last piece into her mouth and was revelling in its sugary sweetness when Harry returned.

'Good?' he said, smiling at her then reaching forward and touching her cheek with his forefinger. As she leaned back—too late to avoid that gentle caress—he held out the finger to show her the dollop of cream he'd rescued from her cheek.

'Oh!'

But as he licked the cream from his finger an internal 'oh' happened—an 'oh' as if someone had touched an old, forgotten bruise deep inside her and she wasn't certain if what she felt was pain or pleasure.

'Have another,' Harry said, pushing the box towards her so casually she knew she shouldn't have been affected by him licking her cream off his finger. It meant nothing.

'Did you like America?'

It was a desperation question—an attempt on Steph's part to regain a little bit of stability in a life that had tilted off its axis since Harry's arrival in the clinic the previous night.

'Loved it,' he said. 'It's so big and beautiful, a bit brash in some ways, but so varied it's like travelling through a lot of different countries.'

He spoke of Boston, where he'd spent most time, and the mountains in Colorado where he'd walked in the summer break. Spoke of friends, the lack of names suggesting they might be women, but of course Harry would have had women friends.

And lovers...

Hadn't he always?

'And Europe? You went back there after your stay in the States.'

She saw the shadows cross his face.

'Yes, I went back there,' he said, then, as the bell rang to tell them a patient had arrived, he changed the subject with an almost abrupt, 'I'll go. You take a decent break. Have another doughnut.'

It didn't take a genius to know he'd been pleased by the interruption, which made Steph wonder what had happened to Harry in Europe. A disastrous love affair?

It hurt the bruised part inside Steph to think of Harry hurting, especially as she'd hurt him once herself.

Hurt him more than once...

Another ring summoned her back to work and she drained her coffee, then chose a doughnut with chocolate icing, taking a quick bite of it to keep her going until the next break.

It was the last bite of the night. She was seeing out the patient she'd been summoned for—a twenty-year-old with an acute asthma attack who'd been put on a nebuliser until the attack eased—when the screech of tearing metal brought all the staff to the door of the clinic. Almost immediately outside, a car had mounted the kerb, dislodging a parking meter then slamming into the window of the opal shop next door.

'Don't go rushing out there!' Harry said, grabbing Steph's arm as she was running towards the car. 'It could be a ram raid. They could be armed.'

'They could also be injured.' Steph wrenched her arm free and continued on her way.

Peter was already at the car, trying to open the passenger side door while the opal shop alarms were making so much noise it was a wonder they weren't all deafened.

Perhaps realising no one was about to leap from the car and grab jewellery from the shop window, Harry had followed Steph to the driver's side, but the engine had concertinaed the car's interior and it was impossible to open the door.

Peter had his side open and was kneeling beside the unconscious woman passenger, while Rebecca appeared in the clinic doorway to let them know she'd phoned for an ambulance.

'There's no obvious bleeding but I guess we shouldn't move her.' Peter made way for Harry, and at that moment the police arrived, their flashing red lights turning the street into a macabre movie set.

Two tow trucks beat the ambulance to the scene, but not by much, and with so many people now milling around, Steph sent Peter back to the clinic but remained close by in case she was needed.

With infinite care, the paramedics from the ambulance first braced the woman's neck and back, then lifted her onto a waiting trolley. Her airway and breathing were checked, then her body scanned for any external bleeding before her blood pressure was taken and fluid lines were inserted.

Meanwhile, the police were assisting another attendant who was using cutting tools to free the driver. Harry stood behind them, watching carefully, and Steph could see that the man must have been thrown forward into the windscreen by the impact, for his face was a mask of blood.

'No damned seat belt—when will people learn?'

Harry had left the experts to their job and joined her on the sidelines.

'If his face hit the windscreen, his chest hit the steering-wheel with equal force. He could have internal bleeding, lung damage, even a ruptured aorta.'

Harry looked so fierce for a moment Steph thought he might say 'Serve him right', but all he did was nod acknowledgement of her recital of the injuries A and E doctors would check first.

Although the action had seemed to be taking place in slow motion, it was only fifteen minutes later that the ambulance with its two comatose patients departed. The police photographed the scene, more flashes of bright light, then a tow truck hooked up to the back of the vehicle and, unable to lift it beneath the shop awnings, towed it off the footpath. As it bumped over the kerb, the back door, released as the car body stretched under tow, flew open and Steph saw the crumpled figure on the floor behind the seats, the long blonde hair pink in the turning light, but so familiar a scream of utter despair erupted from her throat.

All motion ceased, then she was flying towards the car, Harry's footsteps thudding behind her.

'It's not Fanny,' he said, reaching out and grabbing her shoulders, while a policeman moved in front of her to peer into the car.

It *wasn't* Fanny, but the little girl was dead, though she and Harry refused to acknowledge it, performing CPR on the small body until another ambulance arrived.

As it drove away, Harry put his arm around Steph's shoulders and led her back into the clinic.

'We should have looked,' she whispered brokenly. 'If we'd seen her earlier we might have been able to save her.'

'We wouldn't have seen her,' he reminded her. 'The front seat was jammed right back there. She was thrown forward by the impact and I think her neck was probably broken when she hit the seat. Poor wee mite—killed by the carelessness of parents who didn't strap her in.'

Inside the clinic, the various members of the day staff had arrived and were all now clustered in the waiting room, hearing about the early morning excitement.

Harry steered Steph past them, into the tearoom, where her half-eaten doughnut mocked her from the table.

'Get your bag, I'm taking you home,' he said, and she nodded, her mind and body so numb she was pleased to have someone else making decisions for her.

But her limbs had forgotten how to move, and she stood there, her body tight with remembered fear, until Harry took her in his arms, tucked her in close to his warmth, massaging life back into the muscles of her neck and shoulders, softening the tension that had paralysed her.

Her body relaxed—and with the relaxation came tentative flutters of awareness, like the tiny tendrils of a delicate new vine reaching out in search of support.

And finding support in Harry's strong but loose-limbed body.

Surely not...

'OK?' Harry murmured, and she was so startled by his voice she lifted her head from where it had nestled itself on his shoulder and looked into his concerned brown eyes.

'I think so,' she managed to say, though the words stumbled from her lips and she knew she must be frowning as she tried to make sense of her reaction to being held by Harry.

'Maybe this will help,' he murmured, his gaze holding hers as he bent his head a little closer and kissed her firmly on the lips.

Steph was stunned by both the kiss and the effect it had on her, so much so that she couldn't respond immediately. Then, by the time she'd realised how pleasant being kissed by Harry was, and was considering kissing him back, it was too late. He'd not only lifted his head, but he'd stepped away from her, and her body no longer had his support or warmth.

'Come on, I'll take you home,' he said, his voice so devoid of emotion she knew he hadn't felt a darned thing—either from holding her in his arms, or from the kiss.

He escorted her, close but not touching, out to his car, but instead of turning towards her place, Harry drove in a different direction. She wanted to ask why, but she was still shaken by the accident, not to mention the tendrils and the kiss, and didn't want to make a fool of herself by stumbling over the question.

'I drove down here the other morning, and noticed Albert's is still in business,' he said, calmly explaining what she needed to know. 'You're in no fit state to face Fanny if she wakes early. We'll stop there, have a big greasy breakfast and talk about it. You know it's the only way to get the images out of your head.'

Steph knew he was right, even though images of the accident were no longer in the forefront of her mind. But she didn't want someone else—even Harry—being responsible for her well-being. It was the kind of thing she might come to rely on, and once that happened, hurt followed.

'I'll probably throw up after a big greasy breakfast,'

she told him, attempting to negate the 'being looked after' feeling.

'I'll take the risk,' Harry said. 'I'd go so far as to hold your head if you like.'

'Yuck!' Steph retorted, but she had to admit that even an asinine conversation like this had diminished the effect of the kiss—which had, itself, lessened the impact of the accident.

Of course, walking into Albert's brought on a whole new set of problems. She, Martin and Harry had often breakfasted there, usually when they'd been staying at the Quayles' for study week, and a night of study had been rewarded with breakfast at Albert's.

But they'd eaten there at other times—at the end of a night of celebration, often with the people they'd been seeing at the time—and because Albert's hadn't changed at all, the memories came crowding back.

'Bad choice?' Harry asked, picking up on her ambivalence.

'No,' she said firmly. 'Admittedly I haven't been here for years, but we had good times here, Harry, and I'm entitled to remember those.'

Albert himself was nowhere in sight, and the young man behind the long counter was a stranger. So, with his arm once again around her shoulder, Harry led Steph to a booth at one side of the café, waited until she'd slid into the seat, then crossed the room to order two breakfast specials.

By concentrating on the mundane he could—almost— forget the kiss. How could he have been so stupid as to kiss her when she was so prickly and antagonistic towards him? It had been odds on she'd respond the way she had.

With no response at all!

Hell, slapping his face would have been better—at least it would have shown she felt something!

He took the pot of coffee the young man offered, and two mugs, and returned to the table, back in his role of supportive friend, even if it was a friend she treated with suspicion.

'You're off duty till Monday, so will you risk another coffee?'

He waved the pot in Steph's direction and she nodded.

'I think I need it. I'm sorry I made such a spectacle of myself,' she said, pouring sugar into the mug, speaking of the accident not the kiss—she hoped he hadn't picked up on her reaction to the kiss. 'But I thought of Fanny.'

Harry covered her hand with his.

'Of course you did, and you didn't make a spectacle of yourself. You reacted as any parent would. I had a terrible wrenching feeling myself when I saw her.'

Steph smiled at him, because she believed him, and her hand felt good in his, and it was so nice to be with Harry again—to have a friend when she really needed one.

But beneath this very thin veneer of comfort lurked so many black holes of doubt she knew it wasn't wise to relax.

Perhaps she could risk it for a short time—just while they had breakfast together…

Not when you reacted to him the way you did back there! Talk about lurking danger…

Harry watched her thoughts reflected in her eyes and knew she was debating how far she could allow this truce to continue. He longed to reassure her—to tell her he would never let her down. But memories of what she'd seen as the ultimate betrayal of their friendship had been reawakened by the invidious position in which he now found himself.

And once again it was a member of the Quayle family tying him in knots.

He was about to make a declaration—'I won't let you down again' were the exact words he had in mind—when the youth from behind the counter arrived with their meals. Crisp bacon curled around fat sausages, eggs nestled on thick slices of toast, and grilled tomato slices added decorative colour to the plates.

'Oh, I hadn't realised how hungry I was,' Steph exclaimed, looking up at him with genuine delight shining in her eyes, so he wondered if he'd imagined the doubts earlier.

He watched her attack the food with such gusto he found himself smiling, for this was the Steph he'd first known—the girl to whom everything in life was fun, exciting or a challenge to be met and overcome.

To find that girl still existed within the too-thin, tired-looking woman was immensely encouraging, and with a sense of wonder, mixed with a leavening of almost fearful despair, he realised he still loved her.

Shocked almost numb by this revelation, he picked up his knife and fork and tried to concentrate on his meal. Something must have worked, for as Steph's fork flashed across the table to stab at one of his pieces of bacon, he automatically pinned it to the plate with his knife.

'Ask nicely,' he said, looking up and seeing a glimpse of laughter in her eyes, soon washed away by a sadness so deep it caught at his guts and cramped his lungs.

'We can't go back to those days, can we, Harry?' she said softly, then she pushed her plate away and picked up her coffee, cupping her hands around it as if she needed its warmth and studying him over the rim.

'No, Steph,' he said, carefully placing the bacon on a piece of toast before passing it across to her. 'But there's no reason why the days ahead can't be just as good—or even better.'

She took the toast, studied him for a moment, then said, 'Isn't there?'

He had no answer, but he knew she was ready to go—no doubt anxious to see Fanny and reassure herself her daughter was all right.

He ate a little more while she toyed with the toast and bacon, finally taking a bite before putting it back on the plate as if it were somehow tainted.

'Come on, I'll take you home,' he said, when it was obvious she'd finished eating and he'd realised the fat overload was making him feel ill.

They drove to her house in silence, surprised to find the rain had suddenly eased. By the time he pulled up outside her front gate, a shaft of sunlight had broken through the clouds, illuminating the cottage and its straggly, waterlogged garden.

Harry waited, willing Steph to invite him in, but at the same time knowing the less he saw of her the better—at least until he'd sorted out what was happening with Bob Quayle and found out a little more about why Steph was living as she was.

'Thanks, Harry, for being there for me this morning,' she said, resting her hand on his arm. 'I really appreciated it.'

So there was no invitation for him to resist, but the hand on his arm presented a new temptation. He closed his own around it, then remembered there were too many things he didn't know, so he bit back the 'Anytime!' he'd been going to say. He'd talk to Bob Quayle first, find out what was going on, then come to Steph with no secrets between them.

'Give my love to Fanny and tell her I'll see her soon,' he said. He leant across and kissed Steph on the cheek, feeling the coolness of her skin, smelling coffee and bacon and the faint essence of woman beneath them.

CHAPTER FOUR

BY THE time Harry woke, it was midafternoon, and Bob Quayle wasn't at home or answering his mobile. Restless and ill at ease because what he wanted to do was visit Steph—something he also *didn't* want to do until he'd spoken to Bob—he walked down to the beach, then back through the tourist shops to the apartment block.

As he reached the doors of the clinic, he realised that another answer to his dilemma would be to get Bob's job done as quickly as possible then get out of the place. Once he was no longer connected with the clinic he'd lose the feeling that he was spying on Steph and could start again with her.

At least as a friend, though the nagging ache in his body whenever he thought of her kept reminding him he wanted more.

He walked in to the clinic, introducing himself to staff he hadn't seen before, then made for the administration office, where he pulled out the files he needed—staff rosters, staff wages, patient and procedure numbers, and the figures submitted to the government for Medicare payments. He wasn't an accountant, but he'd looked into the finances and staffing of a lot of practices, both general and specialist, in order to learn about setting up his own. The basic accounting tactic was to look at incomings and outgoings and see how they balanced.

And the books were all here.

There was a second desk in the room, which he knew belonged to a part-time practice manager, but twenty-four-hour clinics he'd known in the past had had full-time managers. Maybe that was part of the problem. The manager—whom he had yet to meet—was overworked.

Looking at the staff-patient ratio, the place certainly wasn't overstaffed so that didn't explain any shortfall in the income. And if the problem wasn't in the income, it had to be in outgoings.

He tracked through the ledgers available to him, and finally found the answer. About twelve months earlier there'd been a big hike in the rent. The books didn't tell him why, just that the rent had almost doubled. Going back, it appeared it had been some years since there'd been a rent rise, so maybe the previous owners had negotiated a long-term contract which had finally expired, allowing the building owner—Bob Quayle under a company name—to charge more for the space.

It was more per square metre than specialists like himself would be paying for their suites at the hospital, but he had no idea of the cost of space in the tourist centre of Summerland, so Harry couldn't tell if the rise was fair or not. But it had happened and had certainly contributed to the decreased profitability of the clinic.

Though if the place stopped bulk-billing the government for patients on Medicare and instead charged patients a normal fee, it would not only make more money but it would pay less interest on its overdraft facility which was currently needed to meet the rent when government funds from bulk-billing hadn't come through. By charging normal fees, it would soon find itself back in the black, and from all Harry had seen, this clinic—or *a* clinic—was needed in the area.

He stretched his cramped, tired limbs, then, mainly because he felt so uncomfortable, checked his watch. It was after midnight and, as far as he could remember, he'd had nothing to eat since the breakfast special.

But far more disturbing than missing a couple of meals was the fact that any number of Bob Quayle's minions, by going through the books as he had, could have seen the problem with the clinic's cash flow. Was he so tight-fisted he wouldn't pay someone to do that? So mean he'd asked Harry to do it as a favour?

Harry wouldn't have minded accepting this explanation, but a feeling of unease told him that was too easy an answer. He said goodbye to the night staff now on duty and went up to the apartment, determined to phone Bob Quayle first thing in the morning.

Bob, sounding excessively pleased to hear from him, invited him to lunch, thus spoiling Harry's plan to visit Steph and Fanny. But the sooner he got his business with Bob over and done with, the sooner he could approach Steph with a clear conscience and no secrets.

Oh, yeah!

The first thing Bob told him, after welcoming him back to the house where he'd holidayed so often, was that Steph and Fanny were expected that afternoon.

'It's our access visit,' the older man said, and there was no mistaking the bitterness in his voice. 'Ordered by the courts and supervised by Stephanie herself, would you believe?'

Harry felt his intestines crunch together, as if reacting to a blow they'd been expecting, but though some of his suspicions were being confirmed, he still didn't know why this apparent animosity existed.

'I've already seen Steph. She's working at the clinic. You must have known that.'

If Harry had expected Bob to look embarrassed, he

was disappointed, though, considering it, Bob had probably lost the ability to be embarrassed very early on—one didn't build an empire the size of his without treading on toes along the way.

'Yes, I'd heard she was,' Bob said, as if the matter was one of supreme indifference to him. 'With some teenager left to mind Fanny. The girl could be on drugs, or having unsuitable young men over at the house. It's a most unsatisfactory arrangement.'

Harry said nothing, though the urge to defend Tracy—who'd seemed on brief acquaintance to be an exceptional young woman—was strong. Instead, he asked after Doreen and was eventually led out to the poolside patio, where Doreen lay on a lounger, tanning her fashionably thin body.

Harry greeted her fondly, remembering how kind she'd been to him when he'd been a student and far from his own family. They talked easily, about the old days, and Martin, and the fun they'd had, but as they ate a delicious lunch, served out near the pool by a middle-aged woman who was obviously a housekeeper, Harry's unease began to escalate.

His mind listed his problems quite succinctly.

First on the list—Steph and Fanny were coming.

Second—there was obviously some ill feeling between Steph and the Quayles.

And whose side would he appear to be on, when Steph arrived to find him drinking fine wine and eating a sumptuous dessert with people she might well regard as the enemy?

'I really should go,' he said, pushing the rest of the dessert away and setting down his glass of wine. 'Didn't get much sleep last night.'

'No, please, stay.'

Doreen rested her beringed hand on his arm, while Bob, murmuring something about phone calls, excused himself and vanished into the house.

'Please, Harry. It's been so difficult for us, so very hard, to lose our beloved Martin first, then to be separated from our only grandchild. I don't know what Bob has told you, but we did hope, he and I, that you might be able to talk to Stephanie for us.'

Did that explain Bob asking him to look into the clinic?

Maybe.

But talk to Steph on their behalf?

Yeah, right! Any minute now she's going to get here, fire killer looks in my direction the very moment she sets eyes on me, and never speak to me again.

How the hell did he get into this situation?

More to the point, how the hell could he get out of it?

Doreen was still speaking, and he tried to follow the conversation, but he suspected either his brain had stopped working or she'd overdone the wine, because not much was making sense.

'Natural she'd be upset over Martin's death, but she could hardly blame us for that. But bitter! And unjust. Unnecessarily so. We'd suffered just as great a loss as she had, worse, in fact, for the loss of a child must surely be the worst pain in the world.'

'Yes, of course,' Harry said, wondering if this conversation was leading anywhere, and how he could terminate it.

'She blames him, as if it was his fault he was killed,' Doreen continued. 'Now she won't even speak his name if she can avoid it, but it wasn't his fault he was killed.

If anything, it was hers, having the baby a fortnight early.'

Harry stared at the older woman, wondering if she could really believe what she was saying. And had she told Steph it was her fault? Or made this opinion clear to her?

No wonder there was animosity between the two parties!

'Here's our little doll—our darling.'

Bob's voice, presumably announcing Fanny's arrival, cut off any hope of escape for Harry and, just as he'd expected, the fury in Steph's eyes as she took in the conviviality of the lunch table cut through him like a sabre thrust.

Fanny, however, was delighted to see him, though she had enough sense to greet her grandmother with a polite kiss, before flinging herself with great delight at Harry.

'Are you going to have a swim with me and Grandad?' she asked. 'Mum thought it would be too cold, but I knew Grandad would want a swim, so I brought my bathers.'

Fanny ran back to her mother, who stood like a pillar of stone on the edge of the patio.

'I really must be going,' Harry said, though he knew the damage had already been done as far as Steph was concerned.

Bob looked from him to his daughter-in-law, then back to Harry, but his face revealed nothing.

'I'll talk to you tomorrow,' Bob said. 'And now the rain seems to be finished, you might want to pop in at the hospital and talk to the decorators about the soft furnishings—curtains and such—you want in your suite of rooms.'

Harry felt, rather than saw, Steph's reaction—the air

between them solid with distrust—and when he turned to say goodbye, the look she sent him, through slitted eyes, could only be described as venomous.

Steph nodded politely in response to Harry's goodbye, but regret ached within her when she saw Fanny's reaction to his departure. Harry was promising he'd see her again soon, but Steph knew it was impossible, and her little daughter was going to lose her Uncle Harry before she'd properly had a chance to get to know him.

But once again she'd been lured into trusting Harry— or almost trusting Harry—only to find him ensconced in the enemy camp.

She moved across the patio, settling into a chair not far from Doreen, a chair, she now realised, which was still warm from Harry's body. Fanny delved into the big bag, producing her bathers, and, knowing the routine, dashed into the little shower pavilion on the far side of the pool to get changed.

Bob was also ready for his swim by the time he returned from seeing Harry out, and Steph watched as the big man and the little girl swam and frolicked in the pool.

'She could swim every day if you lived here,' Doreen pointed out, repeating the words she said every Sunday afternoon.

'Yes,' Steph said, because agreeing usually stopped the conversation.

'Now your mother's remarried she doesn't need you,' Doreen added. As this was a new tack, Steph hesitated before replying, but she could see no hidden traps beneath the statement. 'She's travelling overseas for two years, isn't she?'

'She didn't ever need me as much as I needed her,'

Steph said, ignoring the remark about her mother's travel. 'Especially when Fanny was a baby.'

'You could have lived here. You should have lived here! This should be Fanny's home.'

Doreen's voice became shrill and Steph sighed.

'Let's not get into this conversation again,' she pleaded, wondering for the umpteenth time why she hadn't ever come right out and told the Quayles exactly why she'd refused to live with them.

But it would have destroyed their image of Martin and tarnished his memory in their eyes, and they'd done nothing to deserve that.

Nothing more than loving him too much—and giving him too much.

'She could be such a wonderful swimmer,' Doreen said, and Steph closed her eyes and prayed for patience as the same conversation began all over again.

By Monday evening when Steph left for work, she was tired, uptight and very apprehensive.

'If Harry Pritchard turns up,' she told Rebecca, 'I do not, under any circumstances, want to see him.'

Rebecca looked so startled Steph replayed the words in her head, then realised it must have been her tone as much as the content which had taken Rebecca aback.

'OK,' Rebecca agreed, but the warning proved unnecessary as Harry didn't appear.

Steph didn't know whether to be relieved or angry. She told herself she didn't want to see him—ever again—but she would have liked the opportunity to vent a little spleen by telling him exactly what she thought of him.

Within the clinic, rumours abounded. The clinic had been sold again—it was closing—no more bulk-billing.

So many stories, but nothing changed until the following Friday when, along with a slip detailing what pay had been transferred to her bank account, was a dismissal notice. Alerted by the disgruntled day staff, the night shift had gathered in the tearoom, where they'd all fingered the little envelopes before opening them.

According to the notice, the clinic was no longer a viable concern and the owners had been forced to cease operations.

As from this Sunday! She was to work out the night, and weekend staff would operate, but the Sunday night shift would be the last. The clinic would not be open Monday.

Steph stared at the words, sure there must be some mistake, but loud wailing from Rebecca suggested she'd received the same information.

'It's ridiculous,' Colin, the second doctor on night shift that night, said, staring at his own piece of paper. 'You can't just shut the doors of a place like this. Look at the patients we see, the people who need attention immediately. Where are they supposed to go? Another ten kilometres to the public hospital where they might wait six hours before being treated?'

'You're a far nicer person than I am,' Steph told him. 'I've been wondering where I'll get another job, not where the patients will have to go.'

'I guess I'll go back to the agency,' Colin said. 'They can usually get me night work in A and E at the General.'

He smiled encouragingly at Steph.

'They'd probably take you on as well,' he said, but she shook her head.

'The shifts are all wrong,' she told him. 'I'd either be starting late afternoon, when I'd prefer to be with Fanny, or finishing late in the morning, so I couldn't be home for her when she wakes up. That's why this job was ideal.'

'It's that bloke that did it!' Rebecca muttered, turning to Steph. 'Your friend Harry.'

'No!'

The protest was automatic, but a swirling nausea in her stomach belied her denial. Harry *had* been here to look at how the clinic was working—but why was it any of his business? Who had asked him to do this?

Who were the new owners?

With her stomach churning even harder, she remembered walking into the Quayles' mansion on Sunday and seeing Harry sitting there.

Had the Quayles' vendetta against her reached the stage where Bob would buy the clinic and close it down in order to put her out of a job?

And so force her to take up their offer to house and keep both her and Fanny?

She worked through the night, and by morning knew exactly where to lay the blame for her current unemployment situation. Bob had said something about Harry taking up a suite of rooms in his new hospital. Maybe the hospital would have a phone number for him.

But as she said a tearful farewell to Rebecca, promising to keep in touch, a chance remark saved her the phone call.

'We should go straight upstairs and tell that Harry Pritchard what we think of him,' Rebecca said.

'Upstairs?' Steph echoed. 'Upstairs in this building? Harry's staying in this building?'

'Didn't you know?' Rebecca said. 'No, I guess you wouldn't, but that first night he came in, when he was jet-lagged, he said he'd come down and I asked him where he was staying. Unit seventy-four on the twelfth floor—heaven knows why I remember it!'

It all began to make sense. Bob had built Dolphin Towers and, according to Martin, his father had always kept a couple of apartments in the buildings he built. Bob had bribed Harry to spy on her workplace with the offer of free accommodation.

'You go on home,' she said to Rebecca. 'Leave me to deal with Harry Pritchard!'

Shaking with fury, she made her way into the foyer where lifts served the residential tower. She jabbed her finger on the 'up' button, and wasn't the least bit mollified when the doors swept open immediately. She stabbed at the button marked twelve, and as the metal cube slid silently upward she told herself to calm down—to think through this confrontation.

But a red mist of anger prevented any sensible thinking, and she strode out of the lift on the twelfth floor, looked around and spied number seventy-four. It *would* be the one with the views to the beach and out across the wide Pacific Ocean! Bob would keep the best for himself.

Another button to press but, rather than jab at this one, she put her forefinger on it and held it there.

'I'm coming, I'm coming.' She could hear Harry's exasperation through the door, but didn't move her finger so the chiming bell sound continued to jangle within the apartment.

Finally, he wrenched open the door, and Steph's fury froze momentarily, her heart kicking up a notch or two of pace as she came face to face with Harry's broad, bare chest. Her gaze slid lower. Fortunately, from the waist down, he was clad in an ultra-conservative, blue striped pair of pyjama bottoms.

'Steph?'

His surprise—or mock surprise—reminded her of her mission, and she jabbed her finger out again, this time into the middle of the bare chest. She'd teach it to give her palpitations.

'You slime-ball, Harry Pritchard! You cheat! You traitor! I can't believe you've done this to me again. To think I let you see my daughter—that I told her only nice things about you so she thinks you're wonderful, and then you come back to Australia and muck up my life once more.'

Harry had stepped back, possibly because of the jabbing, but he wasn't getting away that easily. Steph followed him and continued to emphasise her points with forefinger on the slight indentation of his sternum.

'Well, let me tell you, it won't happen. The Quayles won't win, and do you know why? Because you're going to make up for this. You're going to find me another job—right now—and if it means I have to come to work for you in your swanky new suite of rooms in Bob Quayle's hospital, then so be it. But even if I'm only vacuuming the carpet, I work the hours I want and you pay me as a doctor. OK?'

She was surprised to hear this declaration, as she certainly hadn't thought it through to that extent, but if she was surprised, Harry was far beyond that emotion. Beyond stunned as well, she guessed.

Which made it a good time to press the advantage.

'Agreed?' she demanded, then, worried she might be late home for Fanny, she glanced at her watch.

Could it only have been five minutes since she'd left the clinic?

'Let's have a cup of coffee and talk like real people,

not actors in a daytime soap,' Harry suggested. 'The kitchen's this way.'

He walked away and she had the choice of following—which was the only way she could push through to his agreement to her demands—or not following, which would get her precisely nowhere.

But she didn't like the fact he was now the one giving orders any more than she liked having to obey.

She went as far as the bench dividing the dining room from the kitchen and stopped there, looking out through uncurtained windows to the still dark expanse of ocean and the brightness of the eastern sky where the sun would soon rise.

Harry ignored her, keeping his back—broad but tapering down to where the pyjamas hung on his hips—to her as he delved into cupboards, producing mugs and instant coffee, filling the electric kettle and turning it on. Then the coffee was made, and he pushed a mug towards her.

'Still black with sugar?' he said, placing a teaspoon and sugar bowl beside the mug.

She didn't bother answering, merely waiting until he brought his own cup across to the bench and settled on a stool opposite her.

'Now, start at the beginning,' he suggested, looking sternly at her. 'Not the slime-ball part but before that. What's happened that you need a job?'

'The clinic's closed as from Sunday.' She shot the words at him, adding, 'As if you didn't know,' with reheated rage.

He didn't take advantage of her short pause, so she leapt back into the attack.

'Just what did you tell Bob Quayle? I presume it was Bob who'd bought the place. Bob, the new owner, identity kept secret, who wanted you to do his dirty work. Only he—'

'Steph.' Harry's quiet voice interrupted her tirade, but he reached out to take her hand at the same time, and it was more the touch of his fingers on hers that made her pause.

She snatched her hand away, but not soon enough apparently, because the sense of warmth his fingers generated lingered on her skin.

'Tell me what's happened. Why you're so paranoid about the Quayles. Why you feel only Bob would shut down the clinic. Why you think he'd deliberately put you out of work.'

Harry's voice was gentle but, as ever with Harry, there was steel beneath the velvet.

She met his steel with a sword thrust of her own.

'Are you saying Bob isn't the new owner? That you weren't working for him?'

'No, I'm not saying that at all,' Harry told her. 'Bob did buy the clinic, and he did ask me to look at it—'

'And you told him it should be shut down.'

'I didn't tell him it should be shut down. In fact, I told him the opposite—that the clinic could be a lucrative investment if it stopped bulk-billing.'

'Well, according to the dismissal slips we all received in our pay packets, an independent advisor had pointed out the clinic was no longer viable and monetary considerations were, regretfully, forcing the owners to cease operations. You're saying you're not that independent advisor?'

'I'm saying I didn't tell him to close down,' Harry repeated, hoping he sounded more in control than he felt.

For a start, Steph had never been irrational, yet there

had been something definitely irrational—close to para-noid—about her vilification of Bob Quayle's behaviour.

But he couldn't let Steph's paranoia get to him. True, there were strange currents flowing here, and apparently the clinic *had* been shut down against his recommen-dations, but for Steph to be imagining a vendetta against her…

'What's happened between you and the Quayles?' he asked again, and saw her reaction in a sudden stiffening of her body, followed by tremors obvious from his side of the bench.

'Steph!'

He had to go to her, to hold her, but she twisted out of his grasp and walked away, ignoring the coffee, mak-ing for the wall of glass on the far side of the living room, where she stood, head bowed and shoulders hunched, her arms wrapped protectively against her body—silhouetted against the magic colours of the rising sun yet oblivious to its beauty.

She stood so still she could have been a statue, long limbs and classic profile carved from the finest marble. The artist would have called it 'Pain' or perhaps 'De-spair'.

Harry followed, but didn't venture too near and though his arms longed to draw her close, and his heart wanted desperately to comfort her, he knew she'd re-treated so far from him he might never get close again.

A matching despair settled like a yoke around his shoulders, but he had to ignore it for the moment.

'Tell me what's happened?'

That won a huff of mocking laughter.

'Where do I start?' she said. 'And why should I, when you obviously won't believe a word I say, even though you've now seen Bob in action? The basic facts are that

Bob Quayle doesn't like to lose. What he wants, what he's always wanted, is for Fanny and me to live with him and Doreen, and he'll go to any lengths, including rendering me unemployed, to do it.'

She turned now, straightening her shoulders and look-ing directly into his eyes, although, with the strength-ening sunlight behind her, her face was shadowed.

'He'd actually prefer Fanny without me—they both would—and that's always the second string to his bow. The moment he gets even a whiff of something that might prove I'm an unfit mother, he'll have a custody case in court so quickly we'll all skid along the pave-ment.'

She paused but only to take in air for the next attack.

'Do you know, he had the hide to have Tracy inves-tigated? My little cousin, just down from the country, followed about by a couple of thugs Bob had hired to check her out? They were too stupid to keep out of sight, and she was terrified, thinking she was being stalked, but when we called the police and Bob explained, it was all laughed off as a big joke.'

'Steph, I hear what you're saying, but is it all so bad? If you look at it from Bob's point of view, would living with them in luxury be so awful? And was it wrong of him to want to know who's caring for his grandchild when you're not there?'

'He could have asked me about Tracy,' Steph snapped, answering the last question first. 'As for living with them, can you really ask me that, Harry? Can you consider, coolly and rationally, the kind of person Martin was at his core, and deny it was his upbringing that made him that way?'

She shrugged her shoulders.

'We both loved Martin, Harry. He was clever, and fun

to be with, and kind and generous, but underneath that Martin was the other Martin, the one who'd grown up with every wish granted, with the money to buy whatever he needed, and the notion that just wanting something was enough to justify having it. Or taking it! The psychologists even have a name for it—entitlement. A person truly believes he or she is entitled to have whatever they want.'

She half turned, so her face was now in profile against the colours of the morning sky, and Harry felt an inner wince again when he read the sadness in her stance.

'Did it never occur to you,' she said softly, 'that it wasn't until you started showing an interest in me— seeing me as a woman instead of a friend—that Martin made his move? He swept me off my feet with all the considerable charm and wealth, and, now I see it, expertise at his disposal. And I went along—fell in love with love, the way he offered it—and believed every lie he told me.'

Her shoulders squirmed, as if shedding the skin of the past, and she looked directly at Harry.

'I will not have my daughter grow up like Martin!' she said, challenge in every syllable of every word.

Then she walked towards the door, turning as she opened it.

'I'll be in touch about the job,' she told him, then disappeared from sight.

He was too stunned to follow—too blown away by all she'd said, particularly her reading of Martin's sudden pursuit of her.

But even if she was right, he decided much later, it didn't mean she was also right about the Quayles. He could see they'd want the best for their granddaughter, so, to a certain extent, he could even understand them wanting people who minded Fanny checked out. But to deliberately take away Steph's job?

She was getting into the realms of fantasy.

Wasn't she?

The questions spun around and around in his head until, by late afternoon, he knew he had to see her—to find out if her fears had any basis in fact.

Apart from Bob closing the clinic, of course.

But he'd have had his reasons for that...

Fanny was playing in the front yard when he pulled up outside, and she greeted him with such delight he swung the little girl into his arms and tossed her into the air.

'That could send her brain bumping against her skull.'

Steph stood at the top of the steps that led up to the veranda, her arms folded, not defensively in the way that said she was defending herself, more defending her home—her family.

'I won't do it again,' Harry promised, settling Fanny on his shoulders. 'Ouch, not too tight!' he added, as the small hands gripped his hair.

'Oh, poor Uncle Harry!'

The child was instantly contrite, smoothing her fingers down his face.

'Can we talk?' Harry asked, as Fanny called to Tracy to come and see how high she was.

'Only if it's about a job.' Steph was obdurate.

Harry felt the frown gathering on his forehead. He was frowning inside as well.

'That's another thing,' he growled. 'The job situation. Not about getting you a job—I'll do what I can to help— but it's ridiculous for you to even consider doing a job you're overtrained for.'

'People do it all the time,' Steph told him, leaning one shoulder against the wall but not uncrossing her arms.

'I know, I know.' He waved aside the objection—and that subject. 'It's the other job I'm talking about. Your GP work. You were always going to specialise—do surgery. You'd even been offered a place on the surgical programme. What happened?'

He could feel her disbelief radiating in waves towards him.

'What happened to being a surgical registrar and working twelve or fourteen hours a day with a new baby? Can't you guess?'

He could, of course, but Fanny was nearly five now.

'But later—you'd already deferred. The Prof would have let you defer again.'

He wanted to add, 'And if you'd been living with the Quayles, it would have been easy,' but discretion was definitely the better part of valour at the moment.

Tracy had appeared, and he lifted Fanny off his shoulders, kissed her cheek, then watched her chase her friend across the yard.

When Steph didn't reply, he turned towards her and saw she, too, was watching Fanny. But the look on her face held little joy—in fact, it was heart-wrenchingly sad.

CHAPTER FIVE

'YOU'D better come in,' Steph said, turning back to face Harry, the invitation so reluctantly issued he didn't want to accept it.

Part of him didn't want to accept. The other part was willing to accept any scraps of time Steph might throw his way. *That* part was desperate to see more of her.

He followed her through to the kitchen, where it was her turn to fill a kettle, pull mugs from a cupboard, make coffee. Only hers was filtered, not instant, made in the plunger he'd given her for her twenty-first birthday.

Martin had given her a car.

Which she'd promptly given back.

Growing up in a single-parent household, she'd learnt to fend for herself—and to pay for what she needed. Her fiercely independent spirit must be part of her war with the Quayles.

'So, tell me,' she said, when she'd poured them each a coffee and pushed his across the table to him. She didn't sit, but leant against the kitchen cupboards, arms not folded, though her attitude was still as defensive as it had been earlier. 'What staff will you be employing? Is it already a done deal? Have you signed people up? Will you be able to find a place for me?'

'Steph!' The protest blurted from his lips. 'You can't be serious about this job. I know you were upset this morning, but don't tell me there's such a surplus of trained doctors at the moment that you couldn't register with an agency and have a job to start on Monday.'

'Not a job that allows me the time I want to spend with Fanny,' she retorted. 'I've been there and done that, Harry. Agencies don't actually care about people—they care about the number of vacancies they can fill. That's how they make their money. Oh, they're charming enough at the initial interview—of course, Dr Prince, we understand completely—and I start off working nine to two-thirty, or night shift nine to five, then next minute the schedules change—they're always very sorry—and I'm paying for extra hours for Fanny to stay late at kindy, which she hates, and I hate, and the Quayles jot down as yet another black mark against me.'

Harry sipped his coffee.

'But I don't see how I can help,' he said. 'I'm setting up in practice—I'll be touting for business. I thought to begin with all I'd need would be a receptionist who can double as a nurse if I need one. I've registered to be on call for the General as from Monday and I'll be happy to do whatever hours they give me, but as for staff...' he tried to lighten the atmosphere with a smile '...I'm hoping the cleaners come as part of the deal with the hospital.'

But if he thought Steph would be deterred by a smile, he was wrong.

'And have you employed this nurse-receptionist?' she demanded. 'Signed her or him up?'

Harry shook his head.

'Not exactly,' he admitted. 'I've spoken to an agency—they're sending people for interviews on Monday. I can't see patients in the suite for another three weeks so there's been no urgency.'

'Until I was made redundant,' Steph said crisply. 'You'd better cancel the interviews.'

He stared at her, unable to believe she could play so tough.

'Steph—' he began, but she held up her hand to silence his protest.

'No, it's absolutely perfect,' she said. 'You're just starting off, so won't have many patients. I can work nine to two-thirty, take my lunch-hour then, and pop out to collect Fanny, bring her back with me to your rooms and she can play there until I finish.'

She grinned at him and he felt an answering smile somewhere in the region of his heart, although his head was warning him things were only getting worse.

'Best of all,' she said, confirming the warning, 'it'll drive Bob absolutely nuts to think he turfed me out of one job, and there I am, working in his precious new hospital!'

'Steph, they're Fanny's grandparents. Does it have to be so—so warlike between you?'

'Yes, it does,' she said decisively. 'And if that bothers you, too bad. You chose your side back when you decided not to tell me about Martin's infidelities, and you obviously haven't changed sides since. But as well as being their granddaughter, she's also your god-daughter, and if you want what's best for her, you'd better agree to employing me—at least while I look around for something with the right hours.'

Steph hoped she sounded more confident and determined than she felt. Inside, she was a wobbling mass of insecurity, made worse by knowing she was hurting Harry, talking the way she was. But Harry had hurt her, and though she was doing this for her daughter, not out of vengeance, a little bit of vengeful sweetness flavoured her decision.

Until she looked into his face and read the pain in his dark eyes.

'Harry, it's not just me!' she said, instantly regretful and pleading for his understanding. 'You said yourself you'd advised Bob to keep the clinic, yet he's closed it—it's a pattern that's gone on since Fanny's birth.'

But it was too late. He was on his feet, and moving towards the front door.

'No doubt you know where the hospital is—you can start at nine on Monday. You'll have to organise furniture, computers, a patient filing system, appointment records, the lot. I assume you can do it?'

'You'd better believe I can!' Steph muttered to herself, already planning on phoning Rebecca to talk about exactly what she'd need. She'd worked in Reception in medical offices to earn money during her student years, and was sure it would all come back to her. But furnishing an office?

He didn't wait for her reply, but he did stop in the front yard to play with Fanny for a while, before kissing her goodbye and promising to see her soon.

Steph felt as if she was being split in half. For a start, Fanny would benefit from the involvement of Harry in her life. In spite of whatever was going on with him and the Quayles, he would be a good male influence in her life. But if she trusted him in the way she'd once trusted the Quayles, was she risking losing her child again?

'It's ridiculous,' Harry muttered for the twentieth time that morning. It was the following Wednesday, and the strain of having Steph behaving as if she really was a receptionist was grating on his nerves. 'A trained doctor ordering office supplies.'

'Get used to it!' Steph snapped at him. 'And bear in mind you're paying me as a doctor, not a receptionist.'

'You must realise I can't afford it,' he grumbled. 'You know the cost of setting up a practice.'

'So borrow more money,' Steph told him, determined to make him pay for his involvement in the loss of her previous job. Then she relented. 'It won't be for ever. I've contacted the agency and let them know what I want. You might be rid of me by Friday, but in the meantime Fanny has to eat and I've a mortgage to pay.'

Harry was caught in a bind. Getting rid of her by Friday should have made him delirious with joy as it was obvious that having her around was going to be so distracting he doubted he'd ever get any work done. But not having her around might be worse.

Would be worse, part of him confirmed.

The phone, on the floor by the wall until the furniture arrived, rang and she dropped down, cross-legged, to answer it.

'Dr Pritchard's rooms.'

Harry studied her while she listened to the caller, pulling a notepad towards her and jotting down words or figures. She might only be acting as a receptionist but whatever Steph tackled she did well, focussing on the task or position with such intensity she was, at times, unaware of what went on around her.

Which had made it easy for Martin to cheat on her.

She'd dropped the phone back into its cradle and was scribbling on the notepad.

'That was Medi-Rentals. From a tax perspective you'd have more immediate deductions renting, but if you borrow money to buy the equipment you need, the interest is also tax deductible and you end up owning the stuff.'

She hesitated, frowned at him, then added, 'Though,

with specialist medical equipment, that's not always good because it needs upgrading regularly, so it could be a false economy. I'll do a few sums and set them out on a sheet of paper so you can compare and decide.'

Harry stared at her. This was not what he'd expected when Steph had blackmailed her way into his office. Though he realised now it was no more than another example of her intensity and focus. He wanted to say something—to tell her he appreciated the effort she was putting in—but the phone rang again, and this time when she answered it her face grew grave and she passed it up to him.

'It's a child with facial injuries—a fractured eye socket from a fall off a bike. Possible depressed fracture of the maxilla as well.'

Steph touched the bone that swept around the nose and held the upper teeth in place, imagining the outcomes for the child if he or she wasn't operated on. She was thinking of how she'd react to Fanny being injured when Harry replaced the receiver and asked his question, so at first it made no sense.

'Did you ask if I would assist? In the operation? You can't just take anyone you like to assist in an operation at the General. It's a public hospital.'

'The patient's been admitted to Summerland Private,' Harry explained. 'That's the first hospital Bob Quayle built—the one close to the beach—isn't it?'

Steph nodded, more intent on Harry's offer than on where the hospital was—although now she did consider the hospital, she felt a shudder of distaste run through her. But Harry's offer was too good to refuse, though in all conscience she had to point out a few things.

'I haven't done any surgery since my first year as a resident,' she told him.

'Maybe not,' he said easily. 'But you've been stitching people up in the clinic, and I've no doubt you can still hold a clamp on a blood vessel.'

He'd been shrugging into his jacket as he spoke.

'Come on. The sooner we start, the easier it is to put the pieces back together and the less likelihood there'll be of infection.'

Slightly dazed, but essentially excited, by this turn of events, Steph followed him out the door, turning to lock it behind her.

'Why did they phone you?' she asked, when they were in the car.

Harry smiled at her.

'You make it sound as if I'd be your last choice,' he teased. 'Actually, the A and E doctor at Summerland Private who first saw the boy worked with me in Paris for a while and knew I'd done a lot of reconstruction work with children. I was talking to him last week.'

In Paris? It seemed odd to Steph, but the closer they drove to the hospital, the more uneasy she felt, and she was so focussed on *not* thinking about the last time she'd been there, she missed the opportunity to ask for more information about Paris.

'Have you been back since?'

Harry had either caught her apprehension, or was mind-reading. He certainly wasn't thinking about Paris!

'No!'

He glanced her way, but said nothing, negotiating the turn into the hospital grounds and pulling up in one of the spaces reserved for specialists. But when he'd turned off the engine, he reached out and took hold of her hand.

'This place had nothing to do with what happened, and if you think of it as where Fanny was born—that's surely a happy thought—rather than where you learnt of Martin's death, it might be easier.'

Steph leaned across and kissed him on the cheek.

'We're still not friends,' she warned. 'You're too firmly in the enemy camp. But thanks for that, Harry. Having Fanny is definitely worth everything that's happened.'

Once inside the hospital, she had no time to think of the past. They were escorted into a small operating theatre usually used for day surgery.

'The two main theatres are being used, but this theatre has been fitted up for cosmetic surgery so will have everything you need. We've called an experienced theatre nurse back on duty and we've an anaesthetist standing by.'

All this information was directed to Harry, though from time to time the woman delivering it—one of the theatre administrative staff, Steph guessed—cast sideways glances at Steph, who, as usual, was in jeans and a T-shirt. Today's proclaimed her to be the sexiest woman in the world—with a huge NOT written on the back.

If this job lasted until Harry started seeing patients, she might have to upgrade her wardrobe—or at least censor the T-shirts.

'This is Dr Prince—she'll be assisting,' Harry was saying, and Steph put out her hand and introduced herself by name to the woman, who was obviously too startled by Harry's revelation to offer her own name.

In the small dressing area adjoining the theatre, more introductions followed—to the anaesthetist and two theatre nurses, all of whose names passed completely over Steph's head as she pulled on theatre garb and wondered if she'd remember any of the surgery she'd once done.

The little boy, heavily sedated and accompanied by his mother, was wheeled into the theatre anteroom, where the nurses took over, positioning the trolley beside the operating table, then gently sliding him across.

Monitor leads were already in place on his chest, and a shunt was taped to the back of his small hand. He didn't look much older than Fanny, and Steph couldn't help thinking how she'd feel if it was her child.

Then Harry slid the X-rays into the light-boxes on the wall, and she stopped thinking of the small person and concentrated on what they had to do.

'We'll cut the skin here, near the hairline, and peel it back. Steph, your job will be to keep it irrigated. Because he's so young and his bones are still growing, they should heal well, but we need to make sure they're aligned properly and check for nerve or blood-vessel involvement.'

Steph nodded, knowing a nerve pinched between two pieces of bone would soon die and the child would end up palsied, like her patient of the previous week. Had it only been last week that Harry had reappeared in her life?

She glanced at him, but he was focussed on the child, and she joined him, keeping out of his way but close enough to be useful.

'If you're not putting in pins to hold the bones together, how do you stop a child his age from damaging his face again before the bones have calcified over the break?'

'We can use a mask. I don't know if they're available here, but overseas I've seen masks made like Spiderman and Batman, even Superman. For little girls there are fairy masks. So rather than bandage the whole face so he looks like the mummy from hell, we can pad the damaged area then use a mask.'

He glanced towards the theatre sister.

'Do you know if they're available here?'

She shook her head.

'Perhaps we can make one,' Steph suggested. 'Plaster might be too heavy, but fibreglass could be used—from the rolls used for plastering breaks now.'

'Maybe we could,' Harry agreed. 'We'll bandage him to start off with, and enquire about masks later on.'

He was cutting as he spoke, separating the skin from connective tissue underneath so he could peel away the upper layer and get at the damaged bones beneath it.

Steph, working close beside him, felt transported back in time to when they'd first qualified and worked surgical rotations together, Harry's eyes meeting hers over the top of his mask. Harry's eyes telling her things his lips hadn't said.

Then Martin had decided he loved her, and had swept her off her feet...

Concentrate! she told herself.

It became easier as Harry began to manipulate the child's fragile bones back into their rightful positions. But the maxilla proved a problem. It was cracked through just below the child's nose, and would need to be plated in order to save his teeth. But though a plate could remain in place for ever in an adult, with a child it would have to be removed later to allow for growth.

'If his new teeth had been right through, I could have wired them to hold the bone in place.'

Harry's voice echoed his frustration. Steph understood he'd been hoping to save the child another operation later.

'No, we'll have to plate it.'

The circulating nurse was sent to find a selection of small plates and screws, while Harry removed some chips of bone.

'How did it happen?' Steph asked the anaesthetist, who'd seen the child earlier.

'Riding his bike, hit a kerb and flew over the handlebars into a brick wall. He was wearing a helmet but his face took most of the impact.'

Steph shivered, thinking how easily accidents could happen, then Harry's arm brushed against hers, and though there were several layers of covering between them, she still felt comforted.

You can't trust him, she reminded herself as she helped him set the plate he'd selected into position, then prepared the skin for closing. But as she watched him place the final tiny staples to close the outer layer of skin, wanting to do it himself to make sure it was perfect, she remembered the Harry she'd operated with before, and the way she'd begun to feel about him—before Martin had stepped between them.

'Done!' Harry said, stepping back and peeling off his gloves with an air of great satisfaction.

The child's face had been protected by layers of wadding, then bandaged to provide more protection. Seeing the mummified look, Steph understood why masks of any kind would be a kinder option for a child.

'You've done that before,' the anaesthetist said. 'That was as neat a job as I've seen in ages.'

'Practice makes perfect,' Harry said, shrugging off the compliment. But Steph caught the 'Unfortunately' he muttered, almost under his breath, and knew darkness shadowed the words. Again she wondered about reconstructive work on children. And Paris.

'I'm going to see the parents,' he said to Steph as they

stripped off. 'Then there are a couple of people here I want to talk to. You can take the car back to the office—I'll phone when I'm done and you can come and get me.'

He tossed the car keys to her as he spoke, and she caught them automatically but, certain one of the people he wanted to talk to would be Bob Quayle who had an office here, she couldn't hold back a protest.

'I'm not your chauffeur!'

She threw the keys right back, hoping he'd miss the catch, but, of course, he didn't.

'No?' he said, eyebrows rising above treacly brown eyes. 'I understood you'd offered to be anything I wanted you to be, Steph. Anything!'

The keys landed back at her feet and, before she could think of a reply, he'd walked out of the room.

Seething helped, but not much.

Calling him names wasn't much better.

And you did offer to do anything—as long as he paid doctor's wages, her conscience reminded her.

Anything?

This time she repeated it with the intonation Harry had used, and an inner tingle of excitement—the kind she hadn't felt for a long time—ran along nerve-paths she'd thought were dead for ever.

Hell! That was the last thing she needed. Harry Pritchard is inextricably linked with the Quayles, she lectured herself. You've blackmailed him into employing you for the moment, and you might—repeat *might*—reach some kind of understanding with him so Fanny can see him regularly, but lusting after him—and that's all it could be—is definitely *not on*.

She drove back to the still-empty office and took out

her bad temper on office suppliers who thought they might be able to overcharge her for their equipment.

'I would have thought your first priority would have been for a practice manager rather than a receptionist,' she told Harry when, obedient to his command, she'd driven back to Summerland Private to collect him. He'd taken the wheel for the drive back, which was a shame as it would have given her something to do with her hands other than wave them in the air, illustrating the extent of the job ahead of them.

'Have you considered bank accounts—patient trust accounts for people who want to pay something in advance? You're going to need at least one other signatory on those, unless you can handle being called out of an op to sign a rent cheque.'

'Overdramatising, Steph?' Harry sent a wry look her way. 'After all, regular payments like rent will be made by bank transfer.'

'And if there's no money in the operating account and you need some transferred?'

'Do it by phone or on the internet. Whoever I finally employ will know the access codes.'

Steph, who hadn't had enough money recently to worry about either internet banking or access codes, pondered this for a moment.

'You'll be putting a lot of trust in that person,' she pointed out. 'Are there safeguards you can put in place?'

Harry laughed.

'I doubt there'll be anything to worry about for the first few years,' he said. 'By the time I've covered overheads and interest, I imagine my receptionist will be earning more than me.'

'But cosmetic surgeons can earn huge amounts of money—and so much of what they do isn't time-consuming. Look at Botox. You could do half a dozen an hour and…'

She stopped, mainly because Harry had stopped—stopped the car! He'd pulled over to the kerb and had turned to face her, then he put his hands on her shoulders and turned her so she faced him.

'Steph, do you really know so little of me that you'd think I'm in this for the money? That I've set up to do nothing more than inject fillers into people's sagging faces, or poison into muscles that cause wrinkles? It's not even surgical work!'

Shame caused a momentary spasm in her heart, but she rallied.

'I thought I knew you once, Harry,' she reminded him, 'and maybe if you'd come back under different circumstances, we'd have got over what happened in the past. But since the day Fanny was born, Bob Quayle has been trying to get control of her life so, seeing your connection there, I can't help but be wary.'

'Oh, Steph,' he said softly, then he leaned forward and kissed her, oh, so gently on the lips.

She knew it meant nothing more than the previous kiss had meant. It had been a kiss of comfort, while this one was more a gesture of despair than love. But her physical self didn't realise that, and excitement buzzed down those recently re-alerted nerve tracks to the inner depths of her body, while the tiny tendrils grew to vines and choked her lungs.

She felt her own lips respond, parting to invite him in, to share the sweetness of the kiss, and for a moment he did, exploring her mouth with a tentative gentleness that teasingly promised passion yet held it back. Then he drew away, leaving coldness where the warmth of his mouth had been—more coldness in her heart.

Releasing her shoulders, Harry turned to stare out the window, then slapped his hand against the steering-wheel. Where had that kiss come from? He'd wanted to protest about her apparent distrust of Bob, but at the same time assure her he wouldn't ever do anything to hurt either her or Fanny. But he'd already, unwittingly, done that with the closure of the clinic.

Although he couldn't believe Bob had closed it to put Steph out of a job...

'What do you want me to do?' he asked, knowing she'd understand what he meant.

'Find rooms somewhere else, for a start.'

He shook his head.

'I can't do that, Steph. I've a particular reason for wanting to work from the new hospital.'

'Because Bob's bribed you with cheap rent? Promised you star billing among his collection of top specialists? Guaranteed you more operating hours than anyone else? Thrown in a free apartment?'

She was angry and he didn't really blame her, but until all the arrangements had been finalised he wasn't going to talk about the deal he'd done with Bob. Especially not to Steph who, from their long friendship, should have known that neither fame, nor fortune, nor star billing had any appeal to him.

Though the free accommodation had been a help...

He started the car and drove back to the new building, parking in one of the spaces reserved for his rooms. The feel of her lips—soft yet wanting—was burned into his brain, and the feel of her bones beneath her skin as he'd held her shoulders was imprinted on his hands.

'I went home and got a card table and a couple of folding chairs on the way back from the hospital earlier,' she told him as she opened the car door. 'I've put some comparisons—buying versus renting furniture and equipment—on the table. If you tell me what accounts you want, and what bank you prefer, I can get the forms you need to fill in on my way to collect Fanny. You'll have to take them back yourself as you have to show a heap of identity papers before you can open an account.'

She climbed out, leaving him sitting, slightly stunned, behind the wheel. He couldn't believe she could behave so—so ordinarily. As if the kiss hadn't happened.

As if she were nothing more than a real receptionist setting up his office for him.

And doing it efficiently, too, as far as he could make out.

He followed her into the rooms, then realised she'd unlocked the door. He had a key on the bunch with his car keys and she'd have used it earlier, but he hadn't given her one for her own use.

As if guessing his thoughts, she held up a small bunch of keys.

'Front door, drug cabinet and staff washroom,' she said, flipping them into the air then catching them again. 'I tracked down the hospital administrator and got them off him.'

She smiled and her eyes sparkled with devilment.

'And guess who was in with him at the time?'

Harry's startled expression must have given him away, for she smiled and nodded, as close to smug as he'd ever seen Steph.

'The man himself—Bob Quayle. But I didn't disgrace you, just tugged my forelock, asked for the keys, bowed and departed.'

'Steph!' The word that had been a plea earlier was now a protest, but she'd turned away and was collecting

a pile of what looked like brochures off the little table
set up in the middle of the room.

'I'll get these out of your way. If you could look at
the figures, and the different equipment the firm offers,
and let me know which way to go, I can order it tomorrow and have it here by next Monday.'

She whisked away, presumably to collect Fanny, then
returned almost immediately.

'You didn't say which bank.'

He named the bank where he kept his personal account, and saw Steph frown.

'Something else that doesn't meet with your approval?' he demanded, infuriated by her nonchalant behaviour.

'It's no skin off my nose, but it's well known their
fees and charges are much higher than other banks'.
However, they may offer more in other ways—perhaps
in overdraft facilities. If you like, I'll get some information on what business accounts they offer and what
the other big banks have that's comparable, then you can
decide.'

She departed once again, leaving Harry feeling dis-
tinctly uneasy. She was determinedly antagonistic in
some ways, suspicious of his involvement with the
Quayles, yet she was doing far more than he'd have
expected a receptionist to do—and thinking further
ahead than he ever had when he'd decided to set up his
own practice.

Steph drove carefully, hyped by the Miss Efficiency
act she'd put on for Harry to hide her reaction to that
kiss, but aware there was so much distraction going on
inside her mind and body that she needed to concentrate.

Queen Street was the main business centre of
Summerland, and all the major banks had branches

within a hundred yards of each other. Checking she had time to do a quick dash down the road before collecting Fanny, she parked and set off, not waiting in the interminable queues but selecting from the assortment of brochures set out for the public to take—brochures which extolled the wonderful benefits of each particular account.

Then to the kindergarten, where Fanny, involved in a game with this week's best friends, was reluctant to leave.

'If I have to leave her here for work reasons, she complains,' Steph said to Patsy, Fanny's group leader.

'Aren't women supposed to be contrary?' Patsy said. 'And you have to admit, Fanny's all woman!'

All Martin, Steph sometimes thought. Capable of not only charming birds out of trees, but charming the trees to do his—or in Fanny's case, her—bidding as well.

'Are we going to Uncle Harry's place this afternoon?' Fanny demanded, when she'd finally consented to leave.

The two previous afternoons, Tracy had been available to collect her from kindy and mind her until Steph had come home.

'We're going to the place where he'll be working, but there's nothing much there yet. I brought some toys for you to play with and some colouring in for you to do.'

'Will Uncle Harry be there?'

'Probably,' Steph admitted, though she fervently hoped he wouldn't be. Perhaps he'd been called away, or he might have gone to see the furniture she was thinking of getting. Although Fanny was showing enthusiastic delight at the thought, Steph knew that the less she saw of Harry, the easier her own life would be.

But life wasn't meant to be easy, was it? Not only

was Harry in the suite but, to Fanny's double delight, so was her Grandad.

She greeted both men with joy, chattering on about her day, while Steph, sensing the tension between the two men, wondered just what she'd interrupted.

The moment Fanny finished a story about a boy who'd called her names, Steph took her hand and led her into the smaller room destined to be a tearoom when the suite was furnished.

'Let Grandad talk to Harry now,' she said to Fanny. 'Here, you do some colouring in while I do some work. We both have to sit on the floor.'

Fortunately, Fanny thought sitting on the floor was something of a lark, so she settled down, spilling pencils from her box, turning pages to find the picture she wanted to colour, while Steph picked up a notepad from the counter by the sink and dug the bank brochures out of her handbag. She'd do a comparison of the various accounts they offered, and let Harry decide.

But though she worked diligently through the information, her heart was racing with apprehension as she imagined what was now going on between Harry and Bob.

A little before five, as she was preparing to leave, packing away Fanny's pencils and discussing with her daughter what they'd have for dinner—'No, you had take-aways last week'—Harry walked in.

'I've taken a look at the figures and need to talk them over with you. The bank options as well, if that's what you've got there,' he said, nodding to where she'd set the bank brochures on the bench. 'I imagine you've still got Tracy living with you and she could take care of Fanny tonight. So how about I pick you up at eight and we have dinner together?'

He must have seen her lips moving to form a 'no', for he continued before she could voice a protest.

'You can take time off in lieu,' he said. 'Tomorrow, collect Fanny from kindy and go straight home. In fact, you could do that every day, and do any phoning or ordering that has to be done from your place. Keep an account of the phone calls. We'll need to set up a petty-cash fund, won't we?'

He smiled, which effectively ruined whatever excuse she might have come up with, because the smile lit up his dark eyes and made her skin feel warm, although she knew he was doing it to silence any argument, not warm her skin.

Fanny, who'd obviously followed at least the first part of the conversation, took Steph's hand and asked, 'Will you wear a dress?'

She then turned to Harry.

'Mummy's got a lot of dresses, but she doesn't ever wear them,' she confided. 'Though I wish she would because she looks so pretty in them.'

'I'm sure she does,' Harry responded gravely. 'Perhaps you could make sure she wears one tonight.'

Steph stopped feeling warm. Her temperature was notching now to hot, but from anger rather than any other silly emotion.

'I don't think being my boss means you can dictate what I wear,' she told him.

'No?' The eyebrows rose above the not-smiling-now brown eyes. 'I'd have thought it gave me exactly that right, and while I'll grant T-shirts and jeans are OK while we're still setting up, I think I'd prefer a uniform of some kind once I open. You'll be seeing to that, naturally.'

Shot down in flames, she still managed to rally.

'Not before tonight,' she retorted.

'Then wear a dress,' he said, making an order of the words, though a fraction of a second later he softened it with, 'Please, Steph?'

CHAPTER SIX

Wear a dress?

Once again Steph stood in front of her wardrobe, and for the second time it was Harry Pritchard causing her indecision.

True, she had a lot of dresses—mostly bought when she'd been married to Martin. He'd loved to take her to the best boutiques and spend extravagant sums of money on her clothes.

So she fitted the image of Martin Quayle's wife!

And possibly to appease his conscience, though she hadn't known that at the time…

She flicked through them distastefully and came across a creamy silk shirt she'd always loved, but which Martin had labelled old-fashioned. And somewhere she had good black jeans—designer jeans admittedly, but at least she'd feel comfortable in them. She dug through the rack of clothes, and found them hiding under a jacket.

Unfortunately, Fanny came in as she was spreading this outfit on the bed.

'Uncle Harry said a dress!' Fanny said sternly.

'I know, sweetheart, but these are good, dressing-up jeans.'

'No!' The obdurate look, which Steph admitted came from her genes rather than Martin's, settled on Fanny's small features. 'It has to be a dress. I'll find one.'

Inevitably she chose a vivid emerald green ballgown which Steph had always hated.

'That's a dancing dress,' she told Fanny, 'not a going-out-to-dinner dress. Honestly, the jeans will do.'

But Fanny was searching again, finally coming up with a slim-fitting black jersey dress, which actually pre-dated Steph's marriage to Martin, and, though old, was so simple in style it was dateless. She guessed Fanny had been attracted by the thin strip of jet and crystal beading around the deep V-neckline, but it was certainly an acceptable compromise.

'OK,' she told her daughter. 'But now you'll have to look in the bottom of the wardrobe to find some black shoes to go with it, then in the bottom drawer of my dressing-table for some black stockings or tights as well.'

Fanny was delighted, crawling into the bottom of the wardrobe and playing there for a while before producing the shoes, then crossing to the dressing-table where she pulled out all the stockings and a number of suspender belts Steph had forgotten she owned.

Getting dressed with Fanny's help took longer than a solo effort, but eventually she was ready.

She studied her unfamiliar self in the mirror, realising how thin she'd got since she'd last worn the dress when she saw the way it clung to her breasts and skimmed down over her hips, suggesting a shape, rather than hug-ging her figure.

And make-up—how long since she'd worn more than a touch of lip gloss?

The image in the mirror made her nervous and un-certain, but Harry was here already—and Fanny had left to greet him—so she couldn't put off her grand entrance for much longer.

Harry, crawling around the floor with Fanny on his back, sensed a movement and looked up, taking in long shapely legs encased in sheer black stockings, then a slip of a dress, a duller, denser black, making Steph's pale skin seem even paler in comparison, and the short red hair even redder.

'You're more beautiful than ever.'

He hadn't meant to say the words—after all, this was to be a business dinner—but they'd slipped out anyway.

'I'm not sure about compliments from a horse,' she said, a slight smile tilting her luminous lips.

Which was when Harry realised he was still on all fours, though his rider had dismounted and was now walking around her mother, nodding her approval of the dress.

He collected his senses, not easy as his eyes kept going back to the silky black legs, and stood up.

'Some dress,' he said, again forgetting it was a business dinner. 'Shall we go?'

He waited while she gave last-minute instructions to Tracy, turning to him to ask, 'Where are we going?'

'I asked the manager at Dolphin Towers. He recommended Travesty—he said it's fairly new and, though it has a funny name for a restaurant, the food's good.'

Steph crossed to the small phone table, pulled out a phone book and looked up the number of the restaurant, writing it down for Tracy. He had a feeling Steph was stalling, putting off the moment when the two of them would be together without the buffer of other people.

But that was ridiculous. She knew she was more than capable of holding her own with him—she'd proved that with the job situation.

'OK, let's go,' she said at last, picking up a minuscule handbag that couldn't possibly hold more than a handkerchief and her keys. She flashed a smile at him and added, 'You've got the brochures and the figures?'

He nodded, because he did have them in the car. He'd taken them home to study them, then, in the process of finding somewhere special to take Steph—preferably somewhere she wouldn't have been with Martin—he'd forgotten about them. But, even though she looked like pure pleasure, she wasn't going to let him forget this was business.

He said goodnight to Tracy, kissed Fanny and felt the delight of her soft plump arms around his neck, then escorted Steph out to the car, careful not to touch her in case the desire building inside him might escalate out of control if he felt the softness of her skin, or was close enough to smell the scent of her beneath the faint beguiling perfume she was wearing.

'I think I'll buy the office furniture and associated necessities,' he said, once settled behind the wheel and determined to damp down the flames with business talk. 'Bob was telling me there's a company willing to supply all the suites at a very good rate, then we can rent the medical equipment I'll need. That way we can upgrade as new inventions and innovations occur.'

Steph ignored the jab of pain the 'Bob was telling me' caused, and concentrated on the rest of the statement. The mix of 'I' and 'we'.

How seductive that 'we' sounded to her thwarted ambition of becoming a surgeon. True, she might not have gone into Harry's sub-specialty, but...

'That was a big sigh,' Harry said. 'Is it so hard to agree that buying furniture but hiring equipment might be the way to go?'

She had to smile.

'It was a sigh for something else—for what might have been, Harry.'

'Surgery?' he guessed, and his prescience caused a

stiffening of her muscles and a prickling of the hair at the nape of her neck.

'Did you do a course on mind-reading while you were away?' she asked, desperate to keep the atmosphere light.

'No.' He glanced her way. 'But it was such a passion with you, I can't help wondering what happened. I know you mentioned Fanny, and understand you couldn't have done your registrar years with a tiny baby, but—'

'I didn't have to get pregnant right then?' she finished for him, hoping she'd learnt to keep the bitterness out of her voice. 'No. I didn't.'

Harry heard the blend of regret and pain and knew there was no way she would regret having had her daughter. But if she hadn't wanted to get pregnant, what had gone wrong?

He thought back, reconstructing the past through new eyes since Steph had mentioned Martin's pursuit of her—and her contention that it had only been when Harry himself had become interested that Martin had swept her off her feet.

All Martin had ever wanted, as far as his medical career had been concerned, had been to qualify, gain some hospital experience in Brisbane, then return to Summerland to run the hospital his father had built for him. Martin had seen it as the start of an empire—and himself as the head of a national chain of private hospitals.

And Steph couldn't have done her specialty years in Summerland. Summerland General wasn't a teaching hospital.

'Weren't you on the Pill?' he demanded, when his thoughts had led him to an unpalatable possibility.

'I went off it for three months—it's what most of us doctors advise women to do from time to time.'

And Martin had been in charge of contraception, Harry guessed, though he didn't say it, merely reaching out to take Steph's hand and feeling the coldness of her fingers although the night, now the rain had stopped, was quite warm.

Steph slipped her hand out of Harry's, but his mind was occupied with thoughts of the man who'd been his best friend. Had finding out about Martin's infidelities affected Steph to such an extent she'd let bitterness colour her memories of the man? That could explain her animosity to the Quayles.

Or was she right? Harry had to admit Martin had been spoilt and used to getting his own way. But had he been devious enough to marry Steph purely because Harry had been falling in love with her? Sly enough to use a pregnancy to prevent her doing surgery? It had all happened so quickly—courtship, marriage, pregnancy— then, in a little over a year, Martin had died.

The problem was, the more Harry reconstructed Martin, the more he had to think about Bob, and being inextricably tied to Bob meant he didn't want to be harbouring suspicions about the man.

'Wasn't that the place?'

Steph's sudden comment brought him out of his reverie. He pulled over, checked for traffic, then swung the car around in a U-turn, pulling up a couple of car spaces past the entrance.

'Thanks,' he said, climbing out and walking around the bonnet to open the door for her.

'Thank you,' she said, and when she kissed him lightly on the cheek, he knew it was for more than his politeness in opening the door. She'd called him a mind-reader, but had she sensed his thoughts? Were the old bonds between them still so strong they could follow each other's emotional shifts?

He rather hoped not, as some of his emotional shifts were practically X-rated.

He took her arm to walk into the restaurant, pleased she didn't draw away, though displeased by his own mental warning that holding her arm was as close as he was going to get.

She was as wary as a cat, and her mood changes as unpredictable as the weather, while suspicion about his involvement with the Quayles was probably providing her with more than adequate armour against any advance he might make.

The tables at Travesty were set apart, small groves of potted greenery providing privacy between them.

'This is lovely,' Steph said, her face lighting up with such honest delight Harry felt his chest cramp with the love he felt for her.

Then she looked at him—really looked—and added, 'You haven't brought the papers—the comparisons.'

Now his chest cramped with a different emotion. She might be relenting—slightly—in the war she'd declared on him earlier, but now she was reminding him this was business.

And that there was a big gap between a truce between them and acceptance back into her life as a friend.

As more than a friend?

Steph sat at the table they'd been allocated and watched Harry walk back out of the restaurant.

He looked fantastic, in a dark suit with a casual turtle-necked sweater beneath it, the dull maroon of the sweater complementing his olive skin and silky black hair.

As well as stirring that bit of her she'd thought dead for ever, he was intriguing her in other ways because though he was, in many ways, still Harry the friend she'd once have trusted with her life, he was an enigma as well.

Driving over here, he'd taken her hand, and she'd known he'd understood, without her having to say the words, what had happened between her and Martin that had put an end to her chance to specialise in surgery. He'd even seemed to understand how difficult it still was for her to reconcile the love she had for the child she'd borne from that unwanted pregnancy with the lingering bitterness of thwarted ambition.

Though he probably couldn't understand her resentment of Martin, who, she was now sure, had deliberately planned for it to happen.

But as Harry walked back in, pink plastic folders in hand, she pushed the past back to where it belonged and smiled, because the joy she felt at seeing him again— spending time with him—superseded even her suspicion of him.

He, however, couldn't be feeling the same joy, because he plunked the folders on the table, passed her a menu and said, 'Let's order then get down to business.'

And Steph, who'd been the one to remind him this was a business dinner, squelched the disappointment inside her and obediently studied the menu, her disappointment soon diminished by the sheer pleasure of deciding what to eat.

Harry had been determined to be as businesslike as she apparently wanted him to be, but when he saw her face light up as she pondered her choice, he forgot businesslike, wanting only to keep her looking as happy as she looked right now.

For ever.

'There are far too many choices,' she finally said, turning to him with her face still glowing with delight. 'What are you having?'

They debated the various options—fish or fowl, meat or vegetarian—finally deciding to share a seafood platter. Well, Harry decided, and though Steph nodded enthusiastically, she had another look at the menu and the glow faded from her face.

'No,' she said. 'It's the most expensive thing on the menu and you're already going into debt to set up your rooms. I know I told you to go into more debt to pay me, but I'll earn whatever you pay me, Harry. I'll do a good job for you. But this is different. Ordering the platter is sheer extravagance.'

He reached out and took her hand.

'I'm not actually broke,' he said apologetically. 'In fact, though I might have to borrow a little money to get set up, it won't be much. I've done quite well, and do have another source of income to back up my own savings, so one extravagant night out won't do any harm. And as you've already pointed out, if things look like they're going bad, I can do more rejuvenation work.'

She shrugged, as if ashamed she'd once put down his business, then frowned at him.

'What work do you mainly want to do? And what were you doing in Paris? Why would there be more children with facial injuries there than anywhere else in the world?'

He hesitated for a moment, then, knowing Steph would persist until she got a satisfactory answer, he told her.

'We, the general public, see the children—and adults, of course—who've lost limbs as a result of exploding land mines—anti-personnel mines they call them—on television all the time. And a lot of specialists and prosthetics manufacturers donate time and equipment to these people. But many of those injured have facial scars and deformities as well, where bits of shrapnel have flown up and gouged out not only flesh but bone as well.'

Her eyes widened, but urged him to go on.

'There's a clinic in Paris where children from the war-torn areas of Europe are brought. The specialists there use a technique of taking bone from another part of the child's body, usually the hip bone, shaping it, then grafting it into place to give definition back to the face.'

'Because kids can cope with a prosthetic arm or leg, but to carry a distorted face through life would be terribly destructive to their self-esteem?'

'Exactly,' Harry said, relishing the warmth of the hand she'd laid gently over his as he'd talked about the children.

'So, tell me more. Does the bone grow? That would be much better than plating or screwing bone together because there'd be no need to follow-up operations. Do you get rejection problems? What are the risks?'

Business was discarded—and any hope of a romantic evening also went west—as Steph demanded to know more and more about the work he'd done. Her excitement shimmered like an aura around her and he realised she'd probably been isolated from this kind of conversation for too long.

There'd been other doctors at the clinic where she'd worked, but only sharing duty with her one night a week, and from what he'd seen of Friday nights, there wouldn't have been much opportunity to talk shop.

So he fed her hunger for information, then fed her

literally, peeling prawns and offering them to her, still talking, egged on by her keen interest.

'No! Eat yourself,' she finally protested. 'I'm going to tackle the sand-crab.'

She smiled across the table at him—a genuine, heartfelt smile.

'I must have sounded desperate,' she said, a little rueful now. 'But, Harry, it's just so long since I've sat and talked medicine with someone—and to hear about the things you've done…' She shrugged. 'I'd be lying if I said I wasn't envious.'

And Harry, who'd always thought of Steph as someone who could have had it all—in fact, when she'd married Martin he'd assumed she *would* have it all—felt the grip of pain for what she'd lost.

'But you have got Fanny,' he reminded her, and was rewarded with a warm smile.

'Yes, I have got Fanny,' she said, and although the words shone with the love she felt for her daughter, beneath that sparkling polish he glimpsed patches of the dusty tarnish of regret.

They finished the meal, then did settle down to discuss business, both ordering coffee while Harry talked Steph into trying a slice of chocolate and macadamia torte as well.

'So, now that's sorted, how are you going to get known?' Steph asked him, licking a last piece of sweetness from her lips.

Harry was looking at her, but the blank expression on his face suggested he hadn't heard a word she'd said.

'You'll need referrals so you get patients. Your savings might pay for the rooms and furniture but for ongoing income you'll need paying customers,' she reminded him.

She saw the little frown appear and guessed he was dragging his mind back from wherever it had been.

'I know a couple of GPs in the area, and now doctors are allowed to advertise—to the extent they can announce they've opened an office—I thought I'd do that.'

Steph shook her head.

'Not enough!' she said firmly. 'You need to join the local branch of the medical association, and there's a specialists group here in Summerland as well. Then maybe a letter to all the GPs in the area, letting them know you're in town but, more importantly, telling them the kind of work you've done, the experience you've had, who you've worked under—things like that.'

He smiled at her and she felt a hot wave of blood colour her cheeks.

'Of course, you'd already thought of that,' she mumbled.

He reached out and took her hand, stilling the fingers that had been playing nervously with her discarded napkin.

'I had, but thank you anyway. Thank you for caring enough to be interested in whether I get patients or not.'

The warmth of his touch burned into her and the urge to turn her hand, grasp his fingers, and drag him across the table so she could kiss him properly was so unexpected she was left breathless—as breathless as she'd have been if the kiss had happened.

She had to get out of here—away from Harry—before more bizarre notions occurred to her.

'I should be getting home,' she said, removing her hand from temptation and pushing back her chair.

'Yes!' Harry stood up, and came around the table to hold her chair, then push it back under the table.

Contrarily disappointed that he didn't argue, she

walked beside him towards the door, going on ahead when he paused to pay the bill but lingering on the path as the sweet scent of some hidden plant attracted her attention.

Drawn to it, she stepped off the path into the shadows, seeking among the rich banks of greenery for the white flowers of a star jasmine—for surely nothing else could be as subtly enticing.

'Hiding from me?'

Harry's voice barely broke the evening stillness, though the husky tones of his whisper caused agitation in her heart.

'Looking for the jasmine. I was going to pinch a bit of it. It grows from a cutting and if I planted it just below my front veranda I could enjoy that heavenly perfume every night.'

'Still a girl who loves the simple pleasures,' Harry murmured, coming closer and encircling her, but loosely, with his arms.

'Hardly a girl,' Steph managed, as Harry's nearness caused the breathlessness again.

'No, you're right,' he said, looking down into her face. 'You're a woman—and all woman, Steph.'

Then he kissed her, and this time she didn't have to tempt him, or even wonder what he was feeling, because this kiss was full of heat and hunger, and it burned deep down into her body, setting her aflame with so much desire a tiny moan escaped from way back in her throat, a moan of frustration that she couldn't press her body closer, feel his skin on hers, find the ultimate fulfilment that was part of being a woman.

A part she'd all but forgotten…

CHAPTER SEVEN

'COME home with me?'

The request was whispered so softly it might have been the rustling of the night wind in the trees, but the seductive undertone, firing need along Steph's nerves, told her it was more than a passing breeze.

It had been so long...

Would it be so wrong?

This was Harry, whom she'd always loved...

He must have sensed her weakening for, with his arm around her shoulders and her body tucked protectively close to his, he led her back towards the car.

The excitement the kiss had generated grew, fizzing in her body like the bubbles in shaken champagne. Speech impossible, she sat, clutching one of Harry's hands while he drove, one-handed, back towards the centre of the tourist strip.

Still clinging to his hand, as if it was the only thing anchoring her to the real world, she stood beside him in the lift as it rose to his floor, then walked beside him into the apartment.

He must have been still unfamiliar with the placement of light switches, for he moved away from her, feeling along the wall, the only light in the room the red blinking of the message light on an answering machine.

For someone in the state she was in, it was a little bit of normality. So much so, Steph moved automatically towards it as she always did at home—when messages might occasionally change her work schedule from week-nights to weekends. As the lights came on, she pressed the button to play then, realising what she'd done—that it wasn't her machine—she turned, appalled, to Harry.

'I'm sorry—put it down to nerves,' she quavered, but her apology was lost as the booming voice of Bob Quayle echoed around the room.

'Have you spoken to her yet?' he demanded. 'It was part of our agreement, remember. Phone me when you get in.'

It was an unmistakeable order and an echo of Harry's earlier words—'I do have another source of income'— rattled in Steph's head.

She stared at Harry, unable to believe he'd betray her this way. Though Martin had betrayed her, and Harry had done nothing about that!

'I assume I'm the "her" he mentioned,' she said, wishing the jagged chips of ice in her voice would tear his skin and make him bleed.

'Yes, but it's not what you think. Steph?'

He came towards her, hands out held as if to grasp and hold her.

She stepped away.

'You don't know what I think, Harry,' she told him, evading his hands and moving towards the door. 'And perhaps it's just as well you don't.'

She was out of the apartment, pulling the door shut behind her, before he realised she was going, and as the lift was still on the twelfth floor, it took only an instant longer to enter it and press the button.

But the satisfaction she felt at the dismay on Harry's face as the doors slid closed was diminished as pain, deadened at first by the shock of Bob's words, now clamped her heart and lungs and made her clasp her arms around her stomach as if to protect her body from an even greater onslaught.

It was inevitable Harry would catch up with her. Taxis were never available when you needed one.

'At least let me drive you home,' he said, standing beside her on the footpath a few minutes later. 'You're being silly about this.'

She turned towards him.

'No, I was silly when I believed Martin loved me,' she said fiercely. 'And silly when I thought you and I could still be friends. Maybe even more than friends. Silly to think I could trust you—trust any man! But right now I'm being sensible. I'm going home in a cab, alone, and that's that, Harry Pritchard. But if you thought you could seduce me out of working for you, well, forget it. I'll be there tomorrow at nine, and the day after that, and the day after that. And seeing you've another source of income—' she let her scorn emphasise the words '—I might not even try to get another job.'

She would, of course, because working with Harry, particularly now when he must know how she felt about him, would be too torturous to handle. But he wasn't to know that.

Let him sweat!

A taxi pulled up in front of her, and as she'd been too busy telling him off to have signalled it, she realised he must have done it for her.

Ha! So, for all his protestations, he was glad to be rid of her.

He opened the door for her and she slid in, then remembered her manners.

'Thanks for a memorable evening,' she snapped, then she turned to give the cabbie her address.

* * *

To say the atmosphere was strained between them at work would have been the understatement of the century, but life was made slightly easier by Harry being out of the office most of the time.

Steph didn't try to keep track of his whereabouts, though she did organise a pager for him so she could contact him if she needed to—or if he was offered some work at either of the local hospitals.

The computer and related software she'd ordered arrived, though the furniture hadn't, but she set up the computer on the card table and drafted a letter for him to send out to local GPs, leaving blanks for him to fill in his experience.

He'd returned the completed letter to the card table, coming in some time after she'd left work, and this became the pattern of their days—she leaving things for his perusal or signature, he returning them when she was absent.

Medical reps started calling, leaving glossy brochures on the drugs and equipment they were touting, often flirting with her, perhaps thinking she would influence her boss.

As if!

No alternative job materialised, so she was still there two weeks later. Furniture and furnishings had been delivered, and Steph began to take a proprietorial delight in the swish look of the suite of rooms, carefully setting the patient files, with their different coloured tabs, into slots in the open shelves, ruling up the appointment book, the day surgery book and the theatre appointments book.

She mastered the phone with its various options for transferring calls, arranged for direct cable access to the internet and had programmes for patient information, pathology reports and medical accounting installed on the computer.

'Have you heard when the hospital will open for business?' she asked Harry on one of the rare occasions their paths crossed. 'I've a number of patients already listed for appointments. I'm to call them back with a date and time as soon as you're ready to begin consultations. And I'll need to know what operations you can do as day surgery and which patients you'll need to hospitalise. Perhaps you could do a list...'

Harry stared at her. He couldn't fault her efficiency— she'd done far more than he'd ever have expected a receptionist to do—but now she was talking as if she'd be here for ever, and being near her, seeing her whenever he entered his own suite of rooms, was driving him to distraction. While frustration gnawed its way through his body, like a lion feasting on a dead beast.

The beast analogy fitted—it was exactly how she saw him.

He'd tried talking to her, and had been met with cold disdain as she refused to acknowledge the passionate embrace they'd shared—or how close they'd come to taking that passion further.

'From the number of enquiries and the people already waiting for confirmation of their appointments, I think you'll need two staff people sooner than you think, but probably an office junior, someone who can answer phones, write in appointments and handle filing would be better than a nurse.'

She continued talking as if the heat thrumming in the air between them didn't exist, but he knew she had to feel it—it was too strong for her not to.

'I was talking to the hospital administrator and he said they supply the nursing staff for both the day surgery theatres and the main theatre—apparently the cost is written into your rental agreement.'

Her lifted eyebrows told him just what shenanigans she imagined had gone into that arrangement, but he'd attempted, over a week ago, to explain about the phone call—and his private income. She'd refused to listen and he was damned if he was going to grovel to the woman.

Yet!

'Hire whoever you think you'll need—or the real receptionist will need. You're surely not planning to stay on once we open.'

'I haven't decided,' she said, but the wide grey eyes with their dark fringe of lashes didn't meet his and he didn't quite believe her.

Steph turned away because she'd never been able to hide anything from Harry. But, to a certain extent, she'd spoken the truth. She wasn't sure about her future.

What she was sure about was that she loved Harry. She ached for him in a way she'd never felt before—with a depth of longing she hadn't realised could exist.

And it made her stupid—running her hands over letters he'd handled, touching his signature as if it could somehow connect her to him.

But Harry had betrayed her—as surely as Martin had done years earlier—aligning himself with Bob, all but seducing her so he could do Bob's bidding.

Though, she would admit honestly, when her interminable musings reached this point, she'd done a bit of the seducing herself. It hadn't all been Harry...

Another thing she was sure about was that she had to get away. Away from Harry. And from any chance of seeing Harry, and, wherever she went, she'd also need distraction—something to keep her mind occupied and fully focussed so thoughts and images of Harry didn't keep popping into her head.

As far as occupation was concerned, she was hoping the decision would be made for her.

That one operation, assisting Harry, had reminded her how much she'd enjoyed surgery and, seeking a good reason to escape a city she now considered too small for the two of them, she'd written to the board which chose likely candidates to take up surgical residency positions as the first step towards specialising, asking if she could be considered.

'You've done what?' Harry roared at her when, in order to bring up the possibility of Rebecca coming to work for him, she admitted she'd made this move.

They were in the tearoom, and she backed away from his anger, fetching up against the sink.

'Applied to be considered for a surgical residency. If the board agrees. I'll take the primary exams next year, and if I do well in those I'll be given a place on the programme.'

'But you'll have to go to Brisbane—or further north to another teaching hospital. And you'll need a general residency while you do your primaries. And you'll be either working or studying all the time—what about Fanny?'

They were in the small tearoom which seemed to become smaller by the minute as Harry loured and glowered and growled at her.

'I can live with Mum and Bill—that's her new husband. Bill was a widower, and he has a huge house with a self-contained flat where Fanny and I can stay. But Mum will be there to take care of her while I'm at work.'

'And what about your house here in Summerland?'

'I'll rent it out to pay the mortgage—Tracy has friends who'll move in with her.'

'Do you want to do surgery so badly you'd uproot Fanny and set yourself four years of really hard work when you'll barely get a chance to see her, let alone spend quality time with her?'

No, I don't, was the honest answer, but she couldn't tell him that.

'I'll make it work,' she said, tilting her chin and daring him to argue.

'Only if you run yourself ragged. And for what? A job that will continue to take you away from Fanny—a job where you can be called in at all hours of the day or night so you miss the important things in her life?'

His voice had softened, as if the anger had run out of him, and he stepped towards her.

'Isn't there something else—something less taxing—you can do? Aren't there other options you could consider?'

He didn't mention the Quayles but Steph could feel them hovering in the background of the conversation.

She could also feel the electricity they'd generated in the restaurant garden still vibrating like plucked guitar strings in the air between them.

'I don't think it's any of your business,' she said, as coolly as she could manage, given the heat searing through her body.

'No?'

The word hovered between them for less than a second, then Harry overtook it, one step bringing him close enough to grasp her shoulders and draw her firmly into his arms. And as his head, bending towards hers, blocked out the light, she knew that not only was he going to kiss her, but she was going to kiss him back.

And the consequences be damned. She'd sort them out later.

Hard, hot and urgent, his lips took command, mastering hers with such effortless ease she felt her boneless body slump against him.

She wound her arms around his neck, clinging to the anchoring strength of his solidity as she responded with all the pent-up emotion that had tormented her for the past few weeks.

His tongue flicked against her lips, seeking entrance to the warm cavern of her mouth. With a thrill of pleasure almost illicit in its power, she touched her tongue to his, tasted him, then let the invasion continue. Trembling now, she clung harder, while Harry led her nerves on an exhilarating dance, teasing first her mouth, then the soft, responsive spot behind her left ear, his moist tongue delving into the hollow at the base of her throat. And when she murmured her delight, silencing her with another assault on her lips.

One of his hands slid under her T-shirt, up towards her breasts, cupping the heavy, swelling mounds in turn, brushing at her nipples until she wanted to rip off her clothes—her bra—and feel those wandering fingers on her skin. Then that torment stopped, and the roving hand was at her waist, releasing the stud at her waist, sliding down the zip.

'I want to feel you—need to feel you, Steph,' he murmured, so huskily the words were like sandpaper on her skin. Then his mouth stopped any protest she might have made, and the clever surgeon's fingers slid beneath the elastic of her knickers, and she shivered in anticipation of his touch.

'Touch me!'

It was an order, and she knew she must obey before

he'd do the same to her and relieve the unbearable tension building in her body. With one arm still around his neck for support, she reached between their tight-pressed bodies, found evidence of how he felt and, with fingers shaking with uncertainty, slowly and carefully followed the outline of his arousal through the fine silky material of his trousers.

The phone rang but, far from jolting them out of their heated embrace, it seemed to accelerate the need for speed—to race to the inevitable conclusion. But Steph heard her own voice on the answering machine as it picked up the call, and the jolt she needed finally came.

She drew back, remembering the other answering machine and the message she'd never clarified.

'What did Bob ask you to ask me?'

The dazed look in Harry's dark eyes turned to puzzlement.

'Bob? Ask me to ask you? I haven't a clue. Dammit, Steph, we're about to make love and you drag Bob Quayle into the conversation!'

Steph stepped away, snapping closed the stud on her jeans, drawing up the zip.

'The other time we got this far—or nearly this far,' she reminded him, 'Bob had asked you to ask me something.'

Harry shook his head. Much more of this and he'd need a holiday in a quiet padded cell. He tried to think back, but his thought processes had been blocked by libidinous overload, and his brain was too busy bemoaning the cessation of pleasurable activities to remember past a couple of minutes ago.

'The answering-machine message,' Steph elaborated, but it still didn't help.

'Oh, forget it, then!' she stormed, spinning around and

stamping belligerently away. She paused halfway out the door, and hope re-ignited in Harry's heart—and other parts of his anatomy. Only to die when she said, 'I've written out a list of the patients who want appointments and why they want to see you. You might go through it and work out if they're day surgery or theatre patients, then write down the time you'll need for the various operations. Then, as soon as I have your theatre times, I can slot them in as possible appointments and confirm after the consultation.'

Harry knew he was frowning—probably ferociously—but how the hell…?

'How the hell can you behave like this?' he demanded when he realised thinking about the question wasn't going to achieve much. 'Prepared to make love to me one minute, icily cold the next, then discussing patients as if nothing whatsoever had happened between us.'

'I can behave like this because I'm a professional!' she snapped. 'Anyway, nothing did happen between us, Harry Pritchard. And nothing will while you're Bob Quayle's messenger boy—even if you can't remember the messages.'

With the new mention of the hospital owner, something clicked in Harry's beleaguered brain.

'All Bob wanted me to ask you was if they could have Fanny for longer visits—maybe even overnight sometimes.'

He stepped towards Steph as he spoke, wanting desperately to get things right between them. 'Would that be too hard to allow? Couldn't you concede them that much?'

But far from getting things right, he'd made them worse. He knew that the instant colour flared in her

cheeks and anger sparked from her silvery eyes like minute glinting arrows, sent to pierce his skin.

'The last time I allowed Fanny to stay overnight with
the Quayles, they took her to Disneyland!'

The bitter words hit him harder than the angry arrows,
but the message they conveyed must have lost something
in transmission.

'Disneyland, USA?' he guessed, to Steph's back as
she was packing up the papers on the reception desk
with swift, angry movements.

'That's the place!'

The words were shot at him with the force and venom
of a snake strike.

'But you can't go there on an overnight visit,' he protested, as the conversation made even less sense the
longer it continued.

'Exactly!' Steph snapped, thrusting the straps of her
capacious handbag across one shoulder and marching
towards the door.

Harry made to follow, but the phone rang again.
Perhaps it was just as well, as he really needed to get
his brain back into function mode before he could follow
up on Steph's accusations.

The phone call, from a woman who wanted information on laser treatment, reminded him of the questions
Steph had asked—about patients and procedures and operating times. He pulled the list she'd left for him closer
and studied it, seeing the number of requests for simple
procedures as well as the appointments for people wanting complex surgery.

Laser treatments and simple procedures for preventing
wrinkles or smoothing out those already present were
more in the realm of a dermatologist, but he knew there
wasn't one in Summerland. Specialist beauty clinics of-

fered a range of these treatments, where trained technicians worked under the supervision of a specialist. He'd have to find out if such a place existed in the growing city, then check out the qualifications of its staff before recommending it.

He sighed. The amount of work in setting up the practice went far beyond anything he'd envisioned. In fact, without Steph, he wouldn't have got as far as he had.

Could he persuade her to stay? Find enough work to justify employing her? Not as a receptionist—she'd already refused to accept the professional wages she'd first insisted he pay her, taking only what a receptionist would earn. But for a lot of his surgical procedures he'd require an assistant, and she had sufficient surgical experience—and was good enough—to take that job.

Perhaps they could incorporate some beauty treatments into the practice's work, treatments a qualified GP could do under supervision...

He shook his head in disbelief at the way his thoughts were turning, but when he considered the alternative— Steph shifting away from Summerland, not seeing her— the inner devastation he felt suggested he should look more closely at the idea.

Steph collected Fanny from kindy and drove home. The letter from the surgical board was in the mail box. With tactful kindness, it advised her their training programme was already full and the waiting-list of doctors wanting to join it so long it was unlikely she'd be accepted within the next few years.

'Damn!' she muttered, scrunching the piece of paper into a ball and hurling it at the front door.

'Bad word, Mummy!' Fanny chided, and, looking down at her daughter, Steph shook her head, acknowledging Harry had been right. Being accepted would mean four years of long hours, hard work and a heap of study. And success would bring even longer and more erratic hours, which wouldn't be fair on Fanny.

'I'll have to get a job!' she said. She didn't realise she'd spoken the gloomy thought aloud until Fanny said, 'But you've got a job with Uncle Harry. And it's a good job, because you don't have to work at night and be tired in the morning, and Uncle Harry likes us, so he'll let you come to my kindy when there's something special on.'

She paused, looking expectantly up at her mother.

'Maybe Uncle Harry could come too, some time. Like when we have a special day for fathers. Remember Grandad was going to come last year, then got busy?'

Steph looked down at the little girl who had her father's eyes, and the familiar cramp of almost painful love she felt for her daughter threatened to overwhelm her. She blinked back tears, and knelt to hug her.

'We could ask Uncle Harry,' she promised, knowing how much the child wanted a father-figure. 'But he might get busy, too. Uncle Harry's a surgeon, so he operates on patients. He couldn't leave a patient on an operating table while he dashes out to visit your kindy.'

'I suppose not,' Fanny agreed reluctantly. Then she shook her head, and with her usual determination, added, 'But I'll still ask him.'

The opportunity to ask him arrived far sooner than either Fanny or Steph expected, for Uncle Harry arrived in person, a little after six, with two plastic bags filled with take-away containers.

'I don't know if you all eat Chinese, but I thought I'd take the chance,' he said, putting his offerings on the table before swinging Fanny into his arms.

'I could have had dinner already prepared,' Steph told him, as her body battled with her mind—one part of her dancing with delight at Harry's presence, while the other raced suspiciously through possible motives for his appearance.

'In which case you could have put it in the fridge for tomorrow night.' Harry's good humour was undiminished by her cranky attitude. 'Shall we eat it while it's hot?'

He looked around.

'Where's Tracy?'

'She's at the library,' Fanny informed him, rolling her tongue around the unfamiliar word so a few too many 'r's sneaked into it.

'Studying with friends,' Steph said, then, as if the words had triggered her own memories, she looked up from where she was unloading the meal and frowned at Harry.

'We shared so much…were so close, the three of us…' she whispered, and he saw the sheen of tears in her eyes.

Harry felt his chest grow heavy with pain, and stepped towards her.

'Steph…'

He wasn't sure himself whether it was a word of comfort or a plea, but she backed away from him anyway, holding up a hand as if to ward him off.

Fanny broke the tension, taking his hand and leading him into the living room where she'd set out the pieces of a large jigsaw. Then, when the meal was finished, Fanny demanded his presence in the bathroom, 'Though I can wash myself,' she assured him.

A bedtime story, goodnights all round and finally

Harry and Steph were alone. He apprehensive, and she, if he went on how she looked, wary and defensive.

'I don't want to talk about the Quayles,' she announced, settling into a big armchair and folding her arms.

Harry nodded.

'That's OK,' he said. 'It's not why I came.'

'No?'

Suspicion lengthened the word so it seemed to echo around the room.

'No!' he said firmly, then he realised he wasn't quite sure why he *had* come. Except that they'd parted badly and he hadn't wanted to have enmity festering between them.

And he didn't want her going to Brisbane, but he wouldn't mention that.

'I came because I've been thinking about your job situation. Not what you're doing now—though you've been wonderful. But a real job. I'll be needing a surgical assistant for a lot of operations. It's not full-time work, but it pays well, and you might pick up other assisting jobs from other surgeons.'

She studied him for a moment, as if trying to read some message behind the words, then said slowly, 'The medical practice where I do a session for pregnant women has offered me part-time work. If I could arrange hours with them that fit in with your operating schedules…'

Her voice was hushed, as if she didn't want to hope too hard that this might actually happen.

'I've been given a theatre Tuesdays and Thursdays, eight to twelve—or later if I need it—for major surgery, all day Friday for day surgery,' he told her, hardly daring to hope himself.

'You wouldn't need me Fridays, then, or Mondays and Wednesdays, so I could safely ask for hours on those days.'

Harry nodded, then saw doubt cloud her eyes again.

'Are there strings attached to this? Is Bob involved? Was it his idea? A new way to bribe me?'

'Honestly, Steph, you're paranoid!' Frustration gave force to his explosive accusation. 'Can you hear yourself? First you have Bob rendering you unemployed by closing the clinic, now you suspect he's behind me offering you a job. It doesn't even make sense. In fact, I think I know why he closed down the clinic and it had nothing to do with rendering you unemployed.'

She looked across at him, frankly disbelieving.

'I went through the books—remember,' he told her, taking advantage of her silence to press the point. 'He owns the building and about a year ago he raised the rent—doubled it. I think he did it hoping the clinic would close. Think about it, Steph. He's building a hospital only three kilometres from the clinic and including a twenty-four-hour A and E service in the plans.'

She frowned at him.

'Twelve months ago? That was before I started working there. You think he didn't want the competition?'

'Exactly! But the clinic didn't close when he raised the rent, so he bought it, knowing he could close it himself. I was just a convenience, really. Someone who bobbed up at the right time whom he could send into the place so it looked as if he'd done the right thing by getting someone from the outside to make a recommendation.'

'I guess if I hadn't talked to you, no one in the clinic would have known your true recommendations,' she said, speaking slowly as if weighing each word.

'And knowing Bob, you must admit that killing off any competition to his new venture would fit with the way he works.'

Steph nodded.

'Yes, it does,' she admitted. 'But though my suspicions about the clinic might have been wrong, my distrust of the Quayles isn't. You haven't been where I've been the last few years, Harry. You haven't had trust stolen from you, not once but many times.'

A hint of tears now sparkled in her eyes, and his heart ached with the love he felt for her.

'Many times?' he echoed quietly, wanting to know more—to understand at least part of her antagonism towards the Quayles. 'Is Disneyland included in this catalogue of betrayal?'

'Disneyland!' Steph gave a wry gurgle of laughter. 'For a long time I couldn't even say the word without a red tide of rage rushing over me. But, yes, that's part of it.'

'So, tell me. Explain. Fanny went for an overnight visit and they took her to Disneyland?'

The incredulity he'd felt earlier coloured the words.

'What about a passport?'

Steph shrugged, then a little smile flickered around her lips.

'I guess, looking back at it, it's kind of funny,' she admitted. 'But, believe me, it's taken me two years to even smile about it.'

This time she sighed, then shrugged again, before settling herself more deeply into the armchair.

'You know Martin and I had been living with the Quayles here in Summerland for the last few months of my pregnancy. It was supposed to be a temporary arrangement, while he finished work in Brisbane, then we'd find a house of our own down here.'

Her voice was stripped of all emotion, and Harry guessed she'd come to terms with the fact that leaving her with his parents had made it easier for Martin to cheat on her.

'After he died, I couldn't go back there, so I went home to Brisbane—to Mum's place. Once a month I'd drive down here so the Quayles could see Fanny, and I'd get into an argument over not returning to live with them.'

She looked across the room at Harry.

'I couldn't do it, Harry. I just couldn't return to where I'd lived with Martin, or risk their spoiling Fanny the way they'd spoiled him. But it didn't stop them asking—pleading, plotting. When Fanny was about two and a half, they started a new campaign. Could they see more of her? Could she stay overnight? My mother had her company all the time, why should they see so little of her? In the end I gave in, and she stayed a few times.'

She brushed a hand across her face, as if the memories were cobwebs she couldn't escape.

'I used to worry she'd get sick and need me, so I stayed overnight here myself, in a cheap motel. Then one weekend I went to collect her on the Sunday, and the housekeeper told me they'd gone away. She handed me a laptop computer and a letter telling me it was connected to the internet and all I had to do was log on, and they'd send pictures and messages every day.'

Harry found the story so extraordinary he simply stared at Steph.

'From Disneyland?'

'I realised that's where they were when I saw the pictures they sent.'

'And the passport?'

'That was my own stupidity,' Steph admitted. 'Some time before, they'd talked about settling Martin's estate.'

She gave a huff of cynical laughter.

'That was a joke! Martin, of course, had nothing, but had conveniently left a will passing everything he didn't have to his then unborn child. The Quayles saw that as his last wish, so told me very early on they'd keep me, and give me an allowance, but that Fanny would eventually inherit their wealth.'

She looked up at Harry, and he saw the hurt in her eyes.

'It was as if they thought I'd married Martin for his money, or their money, and needed to make it clear I wouldn't get it.'

He stood up, wanting to go to her, to hold her and comfort her, but she held up her hand to stop him.

'I got over it, of course, but at the time it hurt—not to mention making me so mad I could barely breathe—and it was then they asked me to sign a lot of papers. It was my own fault for not reading all of them, for signing without checking. The passport application was among them—I signed, giving permission for Fanny to be included on Doreen's passport.'

Harry shook his head. The story was too bizarre to not be true.

'This was two years ago?'

'About that,' Steph agreed. 'She was too young, of course, to even realise where she was, and at an age where people dressed up in costumes rather frightened her. Anyway, after they came back, I stopped visiting. Eventually, they took me to court, wanting full custody of Fanny, citing my work hours among the list of many reasons I wasn't coping with motherhood. They had a top-class lawyer and the battle was horrible, but the judge saw my side of things in the end, though they got permission for weekly visits. Mum had met Bill by then, and really needed a bit of space. Tracy got into the hospitality course at the uni college down here and was looking for somewhere to live, so I bought the house and shifted to Summerland to make the access visits easier. I kept thinking things would get better between us, but they don't. Doreen keeps nagging about us returning to live with them, and Bob—well, Bob's a man who's used to getting his own way.'

Harry shook his head. It seemed unbelievable, all except the last bit. Bob was definitely a man used to getting his own way.

And right now what he wanted was not only more access to his granddaughter—though that *had* been the reason for the message on the answering machine—but also for Fanny to cut the ribbon at the opening of the hospital—the Martin Quayle Memorial Hospital.

He'd only sprung that little bombshell on Harry late this afternoon. Followed, of course, by the inevitable request for Harry to sort it out with Steph!

CHAPTER EIGHT

'SO, WHAT do you think about the job?' Harry said, and Steph, who was still struggling out of the misery of the past, frowned at him.

'Assisting me at ops,' he added.

She knew her frown had deepened—maybe working with Harry she'd get free treatment for her frown lines.

'I'd love to do it,' she said, hoping her inner muddle of delight and apprehension wasn't apparent in her tone. 'But I wonder if I'm qualified—if I've the skills you'll need.'

Harry grinned at her.

'Didn't you qualify as an MBBS? Bachelor of Medicine and Bachelor of Surgery? I certainly did and we went through together.'

'Yes, but—'

'No buts,' he said, standing up and moving across to where she'd practically burrowed into the chair. 'Just think about it. You won't be required to do much in the beginning, and all your surgical skills will come back to you in no time.'

Steph peered suspiciously up at him.

'Why are you doing this? I don't want charity, you know.'

He sighed and shook his head, his dark eyes troubled as he studied her.

'Why do you think, Steph?' he growled. 'Because Bob asked me to as part of some bigger plot? I can understand, because of what you've been through, that you've lost a lot of trust, but you can't continue to let the past colour all your thoughts. I'm asking you because I know you can do the job—and know that whatever you do, you do well.'

He hesitated, as if there was another reason, but maybe she'd just imagined that because now he'd turned away and was patting his pockets, no doubt searching for his car keys.

'I'll see you tomorrow,' he said, and though she knew she had to stand up and walk to the door—see him out properly—she was reluctant to leave the security of the armchair. 'I'll see myself out.'

That got her up, and she followed him to the door, the job forgotten as she studied his back—remembered how it had felt under her questing fingers, remembered the heat that had flared between them only hours earlier...

'Goodnight.'

He'd reached the front door and half turned to utter the politeness. Her body was heavy with longing, and her arm ached with a need to reach out and touch him.

But touching Harry brought nothing but trouble.

She clasped her hands behind her back and echoed his farewell.

'Goodnight.'

Then she stood in the doorway until the red glow of his taillights had vanished into the darkness.

The heaviness accompanied her to bed, damping down the excitement the job offer had generated. It made her toss and turn, unable to get comfortable—to remember how she usually lay to go to sleep.

'Damn you, Harry Pritchard,' she muttered in the darkness. 'I promised myself this would never happen again. That I'd never let a man sneak under my defences.'

And if she felt this level of frustration from just talking to him this evening, how would she cope if she continued to work with him?

But alongside the knowledge of her physical attraction to Harry came the doubts. There was something Harry hadn't told her, and she couldn't help thinking it was linked to Bob Quayle...

Guilt accompanied Harry back to the apartment. Steph certainly had reason to be distrustful of men—of him in particular, come to that. Yet, even knowing this, he still hadn't been entirely truthful with her—hadn't told her he'd offered her the job because he wanted her to stay in Summerland. Because he wanted her near him— wanted to be able to see her, touch her, eventually, perhaps, make love to her.

Adding to the unease was the fact he hadn't mentioned Bob's latest bombshell—mainly because he'd rather Steph considered the idea of working with him without any hang-ups over the name of the hospital. Once committed to the job, surely the name of the hospital would be irrelevant...

He went to bed, but not to sleep, lying on his back staring at the ceiling, wondering if he was being irrational in thinking things might eventually come right between himself and Steph.

Right to the extent they'd become lovers?

Hardly—the way things were at the moment. It was a case of one step forward and two steps back as far as any relationship between them was concerned.

Yet she'd responded to his kisses.

Had almost committed...

He hoped things would sort themselves out soon, because he wasn't going to be much use in an operating theatre if these sleepless nights continued!

Maybe once he'd talked about Bob's latest request, things would get back to normal.

'And just when were you going to tell me about the grand opening ceremony? And faithless Martin Quayle being immortalised in the name of a hospital?'

Steph, with anger redder than her hair flaring out of her like a halo of flame, met him at the door of his suite of rooms the following morning.

Harry straightened his shoulders and let his own anger, honed by the sleepless night, rip.

'When you'd considered the job offer in a cool and rational manner, that's when. Look at you—if I'd told you about the name of the hospital, you'd have gone off into a rage and not even thought about the work or whether you'd enjoy it. And if you imagine I'm part of the plots against you, you're wrong. I only heard about the opening ceremony—and the name of the hospital— as I was leaving last night.'

'When Bob asked you to talk to me about it!'

She shot the words at him, almost stumbling over them in her fury.

'Exactly—because you're so damn irrational no one else seems to be able to get through to you. Heaven knows why Bob imagined I could.'

'Maybe because up to now you've jumped to do his bidding,' Steph said, aware she'd gone beyond bitchy to downright nasty, but so shaken by what she'd learnt that morning she was probably as irrational as Harry said she was. 'The mighty Bob's yes-man!'

She slammed away, taking refuge behind the reception desk, though it was no sanctuary as she could still see Harry, stiff with anger, frowning at her from the waiting room.

She could move behind the filing shelves but that might look as if she was hiding…

A sharp trill from the phone saved her, and she snatched up the receiver, seeing it as a lifeline back to sanity.

'Hi. This is Frank Collins, president of Summerland Combined Services Clubs. I don't suppose Harry's in.'

The outer door had just closed behind his back and, knowing he'd be as unwilling to return as she was to have him back right now, she didn't go after him.

'Sorry! He's in the hospital but not here right now. Can I take a message?'

'You surely can,' the cheery Frank told her. 'Could you tell him we've organised a free flight for his first island patient? He'll be arriving Tuesday of next week. We've accommodation arranged but we'll have to liaise with Harry on details. Could you ask him to phone me when he's got a minute?'

Steph jotted down the gist of the message, asked Frank for a phone number and was given three—work, home and mobile—then hung up and puzzled over the strange conversation.

The man had sounded excited—as if this patient was someone special.

From an island?

Steph was still thinking about it while she sorted through a ream of Health Department forms, filing them away in a bottom drawer in case they were ever needed.

The slight sigh the door made as it closed suggested Harry had returned, so she stood up, startling him as he reached the desk.

He was so close she could see the dark shadow beneath his newly shaven skin and the sheen of his hair where the light caught it. So close she could see unhappiness in his eyes and a grim set to the lips that were now featuring in all her dreams.

She wanted, badly, to apologise, but Martin's betrayal had bred distrust, which was strengthened by the fact that Martin's father now had some hold over Harry.

'There's a message,' she said, speaking quickly to break the tense silence. 'Frank Collins called—first patient arriving Tuesday. I wrote it all down and the numbers where you can contact him. He's at work at the moment.'

She pushed the message slip across the desk, watching Harry's face grow even grimmer as he read it.

'Hell and damnation! I should have called Frank to tell him about the delay. What's today?'

'Thursday,' Steph told him, as puzzled now by Harry's reaction as she'd been by the message. 'What's it all about?'

'And when's the official opening?' he demanded, ignoring her question completely.

'As if you didn't know!' Steph snapped. 'Saturday week.'

'Saturday week—we could operate the following Tuesday. We could do it, but it will be a rush—so much to organise.'

He looked up at Steph and she realised the old Harry had returned. Enthusiastic over something—excited to the point where his eyes sparkled with whatever challenge it was that lay ahead of him.

'It'll take work, Steph. We'll all have to pull together. You said something about Rebecca taking on the receptionist job here. When can you get her in? Today? Then see if you can get hold of a big whiteboard. Ideally, I'd like it in my consulting room, but that won't do for privacy reasons, so find a wall where we can put it. Somewhere we can sit and look at it, so we know where we are at any given time.'

He picked up the phone and started dialling, and when she hesitated he waved her away with an abrupt, 'I'll explain later. The number's ringing—can you switch it through to my room?'

Steph switched the call through, then checked the number of the office supply company with whom she'd set up an account. She was bemused, and puzzled, by the change in Harry, but pleased to have things to do.

Rebecca, she found, would be happy to start working for Harry, and could be in by lunchtime. The whiteboard was also installed by then, on the wall in the small tearoom—the only available space.

'Good idea,' Harry told her, when he returned from heaven knew where and came in to make himself a coffee. 'With it there it hits us in the face whenever we come in, so we can see if there's something we're missing.'

He slumped into a chair and stared at the blank whiteness.

'When's the official opening?'

'Saturday week.' He obviously wasn't aware he'd asked the question earlier.

'Ten days away. OK, write that in up the top so we remember it. Then, in a column down the side, we'll list all the support services we'll need. I've got two anaesthetists lined up and another two surgeons, but I've got to give them a definite date. The kid arrives Tuesday. We'll put him on a strong course of antibiotics immediately—'

'Wait!' Steph held up her hand. 'Stop right there. What kid? What operation are you doing that requires two anaesthetists and three surgeons?'

'Four—you'll assist as well,' he told her, then he ran his hand over his face and offered her a hesitant smile.

'I'm sorry. It came as such a shock to find the first patient arriving so soon—now I have to work out how I can get it all organised in time.'

'Go on,' Steph ordered.

'When I was in Paris, I met a French surgeon who spent part of each year in the Pacific islands. Children were brought in to the larger cities from neighbouring islands and he operated on them. But he told me of the operations he couldn't perform because of lack of facilities and expertise. Children, for instance, who'd had a broken jaw which went untreated, so the jaw healed but with the jawbones fused so the children were left unable to open their mouths.'

'But they'd have died of starvation,' Steph protested.

Harry's smile was better this time.

'No way! Their parents simply bashed in their two front teeth and fed them through a straw.'

'All their lives?' Steph asked, horrified by the idea.

'If necessary,' Harry told her. 'Which is where we come in. The French doctor had tried to organise to get some of these patients to Paris, but the logistics were too great, so before I came home I contacted a local service club who were interested in the project, then bargained with Bob for an occasional charity case in his hospital.'

'You bargained for a free bed in Bob's brand-new hospital?' Steph repeated, aware her disbelief was showing.

'Yeah, well…' Harry said, shrugging his shoulders as if it was nothing.

'No wonder he expected you to run his messages.' Steph barely breathed the words as understanding dawned. 'But you'll need more than a bed—you'll need theatre time, and presumably a post-op stay in Intensive Care for all these special patients, and who knows what other services.'

She gazed at him in awe.

'You talked him into all of this?'

Harry's smile lit up his eyes, then faded as he said, 'Well, I kept harping on the good publicity he and the hospital would get, and I thought he'd finally agreed because of that. But maybe, from the start, he saw I could be useful in other ways.'

'Like being the one to break the news about the name of the hospital—and asking me if Fanny could cut the ribbon?' Steph sighed, then nodded. 'Seems fairly petty—almost negligible—compared to helping a young man live a normal life.'

Shame at how she'd treated Harry swamped her, and she was wondering how to apologise when she realised he was no longer listening, his whole attention absorbed by notes he was writing on the board.

'You know, Steph,' he said, as if there'd never been a moment's antagonism between them, 'it was one thing talking about doing all of this, but now, out of the blue, it's all happening.'

'Except the hospital won't be open next Tuesday,' Steph protested.

'No, but we couldn't operate immediately anyway. We need X-rays and blood tests—need to take some of his blood to store for emergencies. And start him on antibiotics—there's likely to be many sources of infection already breeding happily in his mouth, given the restricted access to it he's had over the years.'

'So where will he stay? Can you organise all of this to be done without him being in hospital?'

'We have to,' Harry told her. 'Hence the whiteboard. I want everything charted on it so we can look at it all the time and know exactly where we are. He'll stay with one of the service club families both before and after the op, but wc have to think about post-op problems and complications as well. He'll need physio to get his jaw working, and speech therapy to teach him how to talk and eat again.'

Harry watched Steph as she considered the magnitude of the task in front of them, and had to hide a smile as she straightened her shoulders. He knew she was accepting the challenge—and doubted whether there'd be any further arguments about her working with him in theatre.

'When will you operate?' she asked.

'Hopefully, the Tuesday after he arrives—that will be a couple of days after the official opening. It's going to be tight for us, but as far as other things go, it's working well as the hospital won't be up to full operating strength and we'll have more access to its facilities.'

'And Bob's gone along with all of this?'

The question made Harry feel slightly queasy.

Or maybe that was lack of sleep…

'He agreed the hospital would take two patients a year—and offered theatre time and all services free of charge.'

'But?' Steph said, no doubt hearing the uncertainty in his voice.

'I haven't actually told him about this patient yet. That he's coming so soon. I've spoken to the administrator—

did that earlier this morning before I called the other surgeons who'd offered to donate their time—but whether Bob knows yet I've no idea. I suspect he doesn't, or he'd have been in to tell me it's too soon or make some other objection.'

Harry suddenly looked doubtful—and very, very tired. Steph longed to step towards him and put her arms around his shoulders—draw his head to rest against her body. But she knew where touching Harry led, so even an exhausted Harry represented danger.

'You admit Bob's in it for the publicity,' she said, hoping she could comfort him with words. 'And coming so soon after the publicity of the opening, it can only be good for the hospital.'

She hesitated, trying to gauge Harry's reaction—which wasn't exactly brimming with confidence.

'Can't it?'

Harry shrugged.

'Who knows?' he said, and Steph felt a tiny tremor of unease reverberate through her body.

Harry had offered her a job and guaranteed no strings attached, but Bob wasn't Harry—and anything he gave free would most probably have not strings but hefty hawsers attached to it.

'Perhaps when you speak to him you can tell him it's OK for Fanny to cut his stupid ribbon at the opening ceremony,' Steph conceded. 'But I won't have to be there, will I?'

'Wouldn't Fanny like you to see her in action?'

Steph nodded reluctantly.

'But it will be from right up the back—not as part of any official party. I know you've been invited to the dinner back at their place later—if they want Fanny at that, you could keep an eye on her for me.'

Harry recognised that she'd been pushed as far as she'd go.

'I'll do that,' he promised, then he took her hand. 'And thanks. Having something to sweeten Bob will certainly help when I spring this other surprise on him.'

He drew her towards him and kissed her gently on the lips, but it was a distracted kiss and she must have recognised it as such for she drew away, picking up a whiteboard pen and waving it in front of the board.

'So what do we write here?'

'Prophylactic antibiotics, X-rays, blood tests, blood retrieval. Let's just jot down things as we think of them, then put them in order and draw up a time line later. Jot down on the right-hand side speech therapist and physio—you might be able to find out who'll be working at the hospital and if they'd be willing to give some time to the patient. And find a dentist—he'll need dental treatment for sure. Then Steve Lowry, Jason Blunt—they're the two surgeons who'll assist—and Fred Carter, who'll bring his own assistant anaesthetist. Their phone numbers are on my desk. They'll need to be kept informed about what's happening.'

'How long will the operation take?'

'Max ten hours, I'd say.'

'Ten hours?'

He smiled at the astonishment in her voice.

'The idea of the operation is to give the patient a workable jaw so we need to drill out the fused bone from the sockets in the skull then fasten something to the rami—those two bits of bone that come off the mandible or jawbone to attach it to the skull—which will fit back into those sockets.'

Steph considered this bald précis of an operation that could take ten hours and saw the first problem.

'But you'll need cartilage to cushion whatever you insert into those sockets to attach the bones and provide movement. Hasn't the jaw fused because the cartilage in the joint either became diseased or broke down in some other way?'

'Exactly!' Harry told her. 'In some cases it's an infection but, according to Frank, in the patient we're expecting—his name's Ty, by the way—he was injured when he was a toddler. He was in a car accident. The car rolled and he was trapped with lateral pressure squeezing his jaw, which obligingly broke. Unfortunately, although the jaw was wired and immobilised, the X-rays taken at the time didn't reveal a dislocation of both sides of his jaw and by the time his jaw healed and the wiring was released, it was too late to fix the dislocation.'

'Too late?' Steph asked, remembering operations she'd seen where jaws had been broken and reset.

'Too late where he lived,' Harry replied. 'As far as I can make out, he was treated by a visiting doctor at a clinic on one of the bigger islands some weeks after the accident, so you can imagine the difficulty in reducing the damage at that stage! It may have been too late even then, but who knows? Anyway, the family took him back home with instructions on how and when to cut the wire. I suppose when he couldn't open his mouth after they'd removed the wire they assumed that was how he would be for ever. They're a very tolerant people, accepting of the troubles fate throws their way.'

'Hmm,' Steph said, wondering if Harry had made the point to remind her of her own intolerance. 'So what exactly do you do?'

Harry grinned at her

'Can you picture the rib cage?'

She nodded assent. 'Sure! One, two, three, four, five and six ribs are attached on each side to the sternum, then seven, eight, nine and ten all join up and are attached by the same...'

'Light dawns? Attached by the same cartilage!' he finished for her. 'While eleven and twelve float free. In fact, the first six pairs are also attached to the sternum by cartilage which gives the rib cage the provision to expand when the lungs fill.'

A familiar excitement began to tingle along Steph's spine, only this time it had nothing to do with Harry Pritchard. It was the excitement of a new discovery—or new to her—in the medical field, the intense delight she had always felt when realising that now more people could have their pain eased or their illness treated more efficiently.

To be part of such a miracle—right there when the surgery was performed—seemed unbelievably exciting.

'You take costal cartilage to cushion the mandibular joints?' she asked.

'We do more than that,' he told her. 'We actually take a small piece of rib—about five centimetres—with some costal cartilage attached. The cartilage is shaped and fitted into the jaw socket with the bone, then the piece of bone is fixed with titanium screws into the patient's mandible.'

'And will it work?' Steph asked, while in her mind she was picturing the different tasks required of the surgeons and the magnitude of what would appear to be a simple operation.

Harry, however, must have been confident, for he chuckled at the doubt in her tone.

'I haven't seen such an operation done, but the surgeon in Paris, who had assisted at one, assured me it will.'

'But the lad's facial muscles haven't worked for years,' Steph reminded him. 'Won't they have atrophied?'

'They'll have had a certain amount of involvement in the sucking movements but will certainly have diminished in size and strength. The good thing is that he's young—fourteen—so there's no reason the facial muscles can't be brought back into first-class working order. That's where you'll come in—supervising the post-op stages and making sure he sticks with his therapy schedule.'

The tingle of excitement she'd felt earlier was now suffusing her body.

'It's better than sex,' she said, beaming happily at Harry, then blushing as she realised what she'd said. It was the kind of thing she'd have said years back, when they'd been such close friends, and not thought twice about—but now...

'Actually—' embarrassment had her stumbling on '—it's been so long since I had sex I probably can't judge, but it is exciting, isn't it, Harry?'

He stared at her for a moment, then shook his head, though whether in disbelief at her burbling comments or at something else, she couldn't guess. With embarrassment deepening to mortification, she rushed to change the subject.

'I can understand a lengthy operation when you have to take bone from another site, but ten hours?'

Harry's scrutiny lasted a few seconds longer, then, as if acknowledging her change-the-subject tactic, he nodded.

'It's difficult because of the proximity of major blood

vessels and nerves so close to where we'll be operating—to say nothing of maintaining a viable airway and transplanting four pieces of bone. The trickiest part will be removing the fused section of the jaw without compromising these, and then maintaining viable nerve paths, so post-operatively, messages will get through to the renewed area.'

He paused, then added, 'Jason's a neurologist. He'll handle that part. Steve will retrieve the bone and cartilage, and I'll reshape it. You'll handle mopping and clamping and whatever else needs doing. The other two will come down from Brisbane the night before, and we'll go over it in detail then. I've already emailed them suggestions as to how I think it will work, and they'll get back to me with suggestions.'

Thinking of the actual operation banished the remnants of Steph's embarrassment. Harry might have kissed her earlier, but it had been a thank-you kiss, nothing more. Right now his mind was concentrated on the job ahead, and she'd better get hers onto it as well.

'I'll talk to the theatre secretary about theatre staff. Maybe two shifts of nurses.'

Harry nodded.

'Unless any of them want to volunteer to do the whole job. Though this is only the first of many patients I hope eventually to see, shifts would mean more theatre staff get an opportunity to see what we're doing.'

'I'll talk to the secretary,' Steph promised, realising she'd need her own whiteboard—or perhaps a small notebook she could carry with her—to make sure all her tasks were done on time.

Then Harry looked up at her and smiled, and she realised the tingly feeling she'd experienced earlier—talking about the op—was nothing on what his smile could produce. But she could hardly take back her comment.

Or let him know how he affected her.

So she frowned, hoping it would look as if she was considering the operation—not Harry's smile.

'You're OK with all of this?' he asked, perhaps more misled than she'd intended by the frown. 'Happy to be part of it? It won't be a paid assisting job, you realise. All the specialists are donating their time.'

It was as if he'd thrown a bucket of cold water over her.

'Oh, Harry,' she whispered, her voice breaking as she said his name. 'Have I really changed so much you could ask that? Grown so bitter you see me as someone who's only out for money?'

She stood up and walked out the door, not stopping until she was out of the rooms and into the security of the staff washrooms, where she locked herself into a cubicle and cried.

One step forward and twenty-five steps back, Harry thought as he sat and studied the whiteboard. How had he come to say something so stupid and hurtful to Steph? Especially when she'd been so excited.

Actually, it had been because she'd been so excited, he realised. When she'd come out with her 'It's better than sex' statement his mind had fought the implications of the analogy for a split second, then had weakened and started thinking how pleasurable it would be to prove her wrong.

True, he'd managed to carry on his explanation of the operation—and hopefully had sounded more involved than he'd felt—but his body had been reminding him of the passion of her kisses and the sweet softness of her full breasts pressed against his chest.

He'd been stupid to think they could work together. She was so damn distracting he should have applauded her suggestion of a move to Brisbane—though maybe migration to Mars would have been better...

He groaned, then studied the mostly blank board in front of him. Today was Thursday and Ty arrived on Tuesday. Well, at least for the next few weeks he'd be too busy to be having libidinous thoughts about Stephanie Prince.

CHAPTER NINE

THE arrival of the young man from the small Pacific island brought a buzz of excitement to the suite of rooms and seemingly to the hospital itself, as more and more staff moved in prior to the official opening.

'We're like guinea pigs for all the different departments,' Steph said to Harry early on Friday evening—the day before the official opening—when she'd returned to the rooms after her pregnant women's session to tie up some loose ends. 'Ty's are the first X-rays the X-ray department has taken, and his blood is the first taken in the new pathology lab.'

She was slotting the X-rays into viewing boxes in Harry's treatment room as she spoke, and he was standing close beside her, peering at the illuminated images.

'Blood tests today are clear of any infection, and the lab couldn't find anything that might suggest delaying the op,' she continued, bringing him up to date on the latest tests.

She stepped back, because being so close to Harry, even when he seemed utterly unaware of her presence, made her feel edgy—even unpredictable. It was as if she couldn't trust her body to believe this was neither the time nor the place to fling itself into his arms.

'And they certainly tried. They took about six vials of blood from the poor lad.'

Harry unclipped the X-rays and slotted them back into their envelope, turning towards her as he did so.

'You've seen more of him than anyone, apart from his host family. How do you think he's coping?'

'I'm guessing he must be apprehensive, but he hides it well. He's behaving like a typical teenager, eager to see everything at once—now! I've talked to him about the op itself, and the aftermath, but he brushes it all aside, saying he's too busy to think about it now. Well, that's what he's jotting down on notes to me, but you don't pick up intonations from notes, do you?'

She was looking puzzled, and a little anxious, as if, in spite of all she'd done in preparing Ty, it might still not be enough. Harry reached out and touched her shoulder, intending the gesture as nothing more than reassurance. But the tension that had been escalating through his body as they'd stood so close to study the X-rays sneaked into the gesture, so it became a caress that lingered too long.

Silvery grey eyes looked into his, asking questions, but telling him things as well.

'Our timing is atrocious,' he muttered, as he used only the minimum of pressure to draw her slowly towards him. 'Has been since I first came back.'

She was within kissing distance now, and hadn't resisted.

'But after this operation—when we know Ty's over it all—we'll be sorting this out. Understand?'

She was so close he could feel the warmth of the air breathed out from her lungs, and her wide-eyed gaze held apprehension as well as excitement.

It was the excitement that made him ignore the apprehension—the excitement that made him close that small gap between them and claim her lips in a kiss, remembering, too late, where other kisses had led.

But this time he stopped it before they went too far,

gently holding her a little apart from him while they both caught their breath.

'We've a lot ahead of us over the next few days,' he said. 'Let's wait until it's over, then make time for ourselves. Time to really think about what this is between us—and whether it's strong enough to overcome everything that's happened in the past.'

Luminous eyes searched his face, and her lips, slightly swollen from the kiss, parted as if there were things she wanted to say. But in the end she simply nodded, then grinned at him.

'OK!' she said, finally putting her agreement into words. 'But shouldn't we have one last kiss to seal the bargain?'

Without waiting for his reply, Steph moved closer, putting her arms around his shoulders and holding his body hard against hers. Then she raised her lips and brushed them across his mouth, her tongue teasing for entry. Harry might not know it, but for her it was a kiss that sealed more than the bargain. It sealed the misery of the past away where it belonged, freeing the happy memories from the clouds of doubt and distrust that had hovered over them since Martin's death.

From now on, she'd remember friendship, and the things she'd really loved in Martin—his humour, his generosity—and she'd open up her heart to Harry so love, if it existed beyond the attraction they were both obviously feeling, could come in.

By three o'clock the following afternoon, she wasn't so sure all the old animosity had been shut away. In fact, if Harry had appeared, she'd have let fly at him though she knew it wasn't his fault Fanny was cutting the ribbon at the blasted opening ceremony. She just needed someone to bear the brunt of her own bad temper, caused by the unbelievably difficult task of dressing a nearly four-year-old for this special occasion.

The dress, presented to Fanny by Doreen the previous Sunday, was so frilled and flounced that Fanny looked like a doll from the top of a very expensively decorated Christmas tree. Steph thought it ridiculous, but Fanny obviously loved it. The first argument had been which shoes she should wear with it.

Steph's decree that only her good black patent leather shoes would do was met with a minor tantrum, Fanny thinking her purple plastic sandals would be far better. This overcome, they then argued over where to tie the sash, how to arrange her golden curls, whether or not four-year-olds could wear lipstick—Steph, 'Definitely not', Fanny, 'But Grandma lets me'—and how late Fanny could stay up on this, her first sleep-over at her grandparents for more than two years.

Grumbling inwardly in frustration over the whole silly business, Steph finally reached the hospital where she handed her child over to an over-excited Doreen, ten minutes before the ceremony was to begin. She waited while Doreen passed Fanny's little overnight bag to the hospital receptionist—doing double duty organising tour guides and acting as a cloakroom attendant—then she wished Fanny luck, kissed her goodbye and walked out the front door.

The podium was set up on the curving driveway in front of the main entrance, with seats, already filling with invited guests, in front of it. Beyond the chairs, staff and other interested observers stood, and Steph found herself a place where she could see proceedings without anyone's head getting in the way.

Which was when she realised she'd forgotten the camera.

'Here! I've got to sit in a chair up front with the other rent-paying tenants. Would you take a photo for me?'

Harry's voice skidded up her spine, causing the little hairs at the back of her neck to prickle with awareness. Steph took the camera, enjoying the touch of his fingers as they tangled in the transfer, all animosity forgotten in the pleasure of just being near Harry again.

'Sure you won't come tonight?' he asked gently, and she knew by the concern in his eyes he was anxious for her—anxious about her mental state on this particular day.

'No, but I'm OK,' she told him. 'With Fanny doing this—with her staying at the Quayles. Even with the hospital name. Martin *was* their son and they loved him and there was a lot of Martin that deserved remembering.'

'Oh, Steph!' Harry breathed her name, and the love she saw shining in his eyes all but overwhelmed her. 'If you only knew how good it is to hear you say that.'

He leant forward and kissed her on the cheek, adding, 'I have to go or someone will pinch my seat, and I promised Fanny I'd be right there in the middle of the front row.'

'You promised Fanny?' Steph echoed.

'On Thursday when she was in the rooms. We had a talk about it and I promised I'd be there for her.'

He smiled and walked away, and Steph, who'd been wondering if things could get much better, realised they could—they had.

The ceremony went off without a hitch—Steph feeling inordinately proud of Fanny. But once the official party, including Fanny, left, the bulk of them heading for the

Quayle mansion for a buffet dinner, Rebecca claimed Steph's company.

'My kids have gone to their father so it's girls' night out,' she said, when Steph protested about it. 'Besides, you've been working so hard you need a break before the real work of Ty's operation and post-op work begins.'

They had an early dinner at a restaurant in the centre of Summerland's tourist area, then, after discussing various movie options, decided a long walk on the beach would be far nicer than sitting in a stuffy movie theatre.

Steph arrived home a little after ten, to a house that felt curiously empty as Tracy had gone surfing with friends further down the coast and would be away until Monday evening.

The message light on the answering machine was blinking, and for once Steph felt no anxiety as the flashing red eye lit the darkness. Though it might be Fanny, ringing up to say goodnight.

She hit the replay button as she walked past, heading for the kitchen and a drink of water.

Not Fanny, but Harry.

'Steph, is Fanny with you? Did you pick her up from the Quayles'? Phone my mobile as soon as you get in.'

Cold dread seized Steph's heart, clutching like an icy hand and squeezing so tightly she couldn't breathe.

Telling herself not to panic, she rushed towards the phone and with fumbling fingers dialled Harry's mobile.

'Of course she's not with me!' she screamed into the phone. 'How long has she been missing? Have you called the police? Or did you just assume I had her and keep on partying?'

She slammed down the phone and rushed out the front door, car keys clenched in her fist because she couldn't trust her shaking fingers not to drop them. The car started, and she summoned every ounce of will-power in her possession and forced herself to drive, slowly and carefully, towards the Quayle mansion.

Police cars in the drive told her at least something was being done to find her daughter, but when a young constable tried to stop her parking behind them, her control cracked and she yelled at him, telling him to stay away from her—to get out and find her child.

'Steph!' Harry appeared from nowhere, but though he tried to put his arm around her, she dodged away.

The fear she'd held at bay as she'd driven to the house erupted in volcanic anger, and she turned on him, flinging accusations at him, blaming his return—his interference in her life—saying things that even in her terrified state she knew were unforgivable.

He stood back and took it all, bowing his head as if to acknowledge her right to this rage, then, when she'd wound down and anger had been replaced by gut-wrenching sobs, he put his arm around her and led her carefully up to the house.

'Are you sure this isn't another of Doreen's tricks?' she demanded, hesitating on the doorstep of the house she still hated entering. 'How could this have happened if she or Bob weren't involved?'

Harry heard the fear and grief that closed her throat, making her voice hoarse and scratchy.

'They are as upset as you, Steph,' he said quietly. 'Doreen had to be sedated and you only have to look at Bob to know he had nothing to do with it.'

He eased her through the door, carrying his own guilt like a weight around his shoulders, echoes of his own promise for Fanny's safety—'I'll watch over her'—hammering in his head.

Steph had let loose her rage on him, but she couldn't possibly berate him as much as he had blamed himself.

While as for any hope of a relationship after this…

One step forward, four hundred steps back, though his personal feelings were of no account right now.

'When did it happen?'

She was looking around the foyer as if she'd never been there before—never lived in this huge mansion.

'We don't know, Steph,' he answered. 'Not precisely. Doreen took her up to bed at eight, read her a story and tucked her in. She stayed until Fanny went to sleep at about eight-fifteen. Then Mrs Woods went up to check on her a little before nine.'

He paused, because his mouth was dry with the terrible tension he felt, just repeating what had happened.

'At first Mrs Woods thought she might be hiding, but when she couldn't find her upstairs, she alerted Bob and the dinner guests helped search the house.'

'Then, no doubt, Bob came up with the notion I'd taken her and you all relaxed,' Steph snapped, as her anxiety overflowed into anger once again so she had to strike out—to hurt someone as badly as she was hurting.

'I don't think we ever seriously considered that,' Harry said, aligning himself with the Quayles with that 'we'.

But at that moment Bob appeared, looking as if he'd aged twenty years since she'd seen him that afternoon.

'Stephanie!' he said—making a desperate plea of her name and walking towards her with his hands outstretched in supplication.

Steph saw his pain—knew it mirrored her own—and took his hands, pressing them tight—comfortee turned comforter.

'I'm going back outside,' he said. 'I know I'm probably useless out there, but I can't bear to do nothing.'

Steph nodded, and watched him go, then she looked around the foyer with its high walls reaching up two storeys, and the grand staircase stretching to the upper floor. She needed something to do as well, because it seemed as if the walls were closing in on her. She bit back a scream of sheer frustrated terror.

Harry must have sensed she was close to collapse. Up to now, he'd been careful not to stand too close, but now he put his arm around her shoulders again, helping her towards the steps, talking calmly, though his voice was croaky with emotion.

'The police are undertaking another search of the house and gardens, while two detectives are in the library. They're taking the names and addresses of all the guests, questioning them about what they might have seen, then letting them go. The guests are in the living room, so you probably don't want to go in there. Would you like to sit here on the steps or go out by the pool?'

Steph shook her head.

'I can't just sit and wait—I need to look for her.'

'Where, Steph?' he said, and she shook her head, feeling the tears of utter helplessness sliding down her cheeks.

'Can I look at her room? Is her bag gone?'

'I'll ask someone,' Harry said, hovering by her side, within touching distance but again not touching.

A harassed-looking man, clad in faded jeans and a checked shirt, appeared at that moment.

'Is this Mrs Quayle?' he asked, coming towards them.

'Prince. My name is Prince,' Steph said. 'I'm Fanny's mother. What's happening?'

'Brad Drew, Summerland CID,' he said, putting out

his hand but obviously not expecting her to respond to the politeness. 'We're searching for your daughter—we've circulated her description. We've fingerprint experts coming to dust the bedroom, and we're questioning all the guests. Two television channels covered the opening of the hospital. We're arranging to get copies of all the footage they shot, so we'll know who was there.'

He paused for a moment, then added, 'I'll need to ask you some questions as well, ma'am. About where you were tonight and who was with you. And about who might want to harm you in any way.'

'No one,' Steph said, but the coincidence of the hospital opening and Fanny's disappearance had suddenly clicked in her mind. Horrified by her suspicions, she grasped the policeman's arm. 'The hospital opening? She was there on the podium, granddaughter of the owners. Could a sick mind think a hospital owner must have money? Could someone have taken her for ransom?'

She knew her fingers must be biting into his arm, for she'd felt him flinch, but the look he exchanged with Harry puzzled her. It was almost one of relief, as if kidnapping was a good option to explain her daughter's disappearance.

But neither man explained the look and she was too distraught to think more about it, asking again about Fanny's overnight bag and if she could see the bedroom.

'The bag is gone—Mrs Woods noticed that immediately. It's better if you don't go up there,' the policeman said. 'Not because the room's upset in any way, but the fewer people we have in that part of the house, the more chance there is of the scene-of-crime officers finding something helpful.'

Steph nodded, and felt her shoulders slump with helplessness.

'But I need to do something!' she said.

'Come into the kitchen and have a cup of tea,' Harry suggested. 'Brad needs to ask you questions—about friends and relatives, about Fanny herself and whether she'd go off with someone she didn't know. You need to put aside your anxiety for a little while and think about the answers.'

Harry's voice seemed to echo in a vast empty space inside her head, but when he put his arm around her shoulders and led her into the kitchen, she went. The way her knees were shaking, sitting down was definitely a good option, and she doubted whether she'd have found her way anywhere without Harry to lean on— Harry to lead her around.

Brad's questions began simply enough—name, address, details of where Fanny went to kindy. But as he persisted, Steph sensed some purpose behind them, but was too consumed with worry to work out what.

'And although your daughter was in the official party at the opening of the hospital—named after your husband—you weren't.' It was a statement, not a question, so Steph ignored it. Then Brad followed it up with a real doozy.

'You've a history of bad relations with your parents-in-law,' he said bluntly.

Steph looked from Harry to Brad, as the undertones she'd sensed in Brad's questions suddenly became clearer, but before she could protest, Harry exploded.

'Where Steph was tonight or why she wasn't in the official party are nothing to do with Fanny's disappearance,' he said, his voice not loud but deep with anger. 'There is no way she'd hurt a hair on Fanny's head, nor would she pull a stunt like this for attention, or revenge, or any other macabre reason your policeman's brain might throw up.'

'You know Dr Prince that well?' the policeman asked, and Steph looked at Harry, who'd turned towards her, his eyes full of worry and pain.

'I know her as well as I know myself. She had nothing to do with Fanny's disappearance, so why don't you get someone onto checking her alibi, if that's what you need to do, so we can move past this to more productive questions?'

Brad made some reply, but Steph didn't hear it as her head was repeating the words Harry had spoken—'I know her as well as I know myself.' For some reason, she found comfort in that simple declaration, and they gave her the strength she needed to keep going a little longer.

By Monday morning, there was still no news in spite of the fact Fanny's picture had appeared in every newspaper and had been splashed across television screens throughout the country. Neither had there been a ransom demand, a bad sign now Steph had figured out what the look between Harry and Brad had meant. To them, kidnapping for ransom was a good option—the only other one being that some sick or perverted stranger had taken the child.

Even *she* knew that a kidnapped child had some hope of being returned…

'It wasn't as if it was a sit-down dinner. How could she possibly disappear from a house with fifty people wandering around the rooms on the ground floor?' Steph demanded of Brad, who was sitting in her living room, going over the situation yet again. Again asking questions in the hope some chance remark or response might reveal a motive for Fanny's disappearance. 'Why choose a time like that? When there were so many chances of being caught?'

Bob stopped pacing by the window and came to sit beside Steph on the couch.

'Whoever did it might have chosen a time like that deliberately,' Brad reminded her, while Bob put his arm around her shoulders, offering silent support and comfort.

Bob had rarely moved from Steph's side, he and Harry sitting out the long days and even longer nights with her. No one saying much as tortured thoughts were best left unspoken.

And though in her heart she knew she needed him near her, Steph had protested about Harry's presence. With Ty's operation only twenty-four hours away, there was so much he should be doing.

'I can postpone it,' he'd said earlier, when she'd practically had to push him out of the house to go up to the hospital to check on Ty's admittance.

'No way,' she'd told him. 'That boy's been building up to this—to postpone it would be cruel to him.'

She'd squeezed his hand and kissed his cheek.

'Go, Harry,' she'd said, and he'd gone.

But his departure had left her with a new sense of emptiness, one that made her think about how quickly Harry had found his way back into her life, breaking through the careful defences she'd built up to protect herself from hurt.

Not that any defence had protected Fanny…

Brad's voice brought her out of her dismal thoughts.

'I've got the films of the official opening from all the television studios,' he told them. 'Our men have been through it and spliced it together so you only have to watch one video. I can play it as many times as you like, but what I really need are the names of everyone who was there.'

He slotted the video into Steph's player and turned to Bob.

'With the help of the hospital admin staff, we've identified most of the invited guests and a lot of the staff, but there are a number of people—you'll see their faces ringed by white lines—we can't put names to. Harry went through it last night—'

'Harry went through it last night?' Steph echoed. 'When last night? He was here.'

Bob and Brad exchanged a look, then Bob shrugged.

'He phoned Brad and offered to take a look at it when you went to sleep last night,' he explained. 'He knew he might not be able to be here this morning and went across to the station at about eleven.'

'But he was supposed to be sleeping himself,' Steph protested. 'You both said you'd sleep if I agreed to take a sleeping tablet.'

'To get back to the video,' Brad interrupted. 'If you could both concentrate on the faces ringed in white.'

Steph nodded, and Brad used the remote to start the tape rolling. She saw a shot of herself, and brushed away useless tears as her beautiful daughter cut the ribbon. The sound had been removed, but as she watched Bob make his speech, she remembered parts of what he'd said, and felt the heaviness of regret that it had taken so long for her to get over not Martin's death but his betrayal.

The first circled head was that of a man who seemed vaguely familiar. Brad stopped the tape so they could look at the fuzzy image.

'Kent Cross, one of the security men employed by my

building firm. I had a few of them there to boost the hospital security numbers,' Bob told Brad, and Steph knew from the hopelessness in Bob's voice he was thinking how useless security had been.

Another man, and this one Steph knew.

'Bill Jackson—he's a local GP who works at the practice where I do a session on Fridays. I didn't see him there.'

Brad wrote down the name, and moved the film on.

Steph saw herself again, this time with Rebecca—head circled.

'That's my friend—Harry's new receptionist.'

'Of course,' Brad said. 'I should have recognised her. I interviewed her myself.'

Because you had—or still have—suspicions I might have taken Fanny myself, Steph thought as the agony of the situation swept over her again. She put her hands to her face, wanting to cry until she had no tears left, but Bob squeezed her shoulder, alerting her to the fact the tape was rolling again.

Another woman—again a sense of familiarity. Only this time the familiarity was accompanied by a feeling of nausea.

Steph shook the bad memories away and waited for the film to move on.

It didn't.

Brad was looking at her.

'You know that woman?'

Steph shook her head.

'She reminded me of someone, that's all. It brought back...'

Remembering what it had brought back, and Bob's presence right beside her, she didn't finish.

But Brad persisted.

'Bad memories? She's someone you don't like?'

'It couldn't possibly be her,' Steph said, angered by his persistence. 'And it's more than four years since I saw her and then it was only once, so I wouldn't recognise her well enough to positively identify her anyway.'

'Any tiny thing might help,' Brad reminded her. 'Anything slightly out of sync. Even someone you haven't seen for four or five years appearing in your life again.'

Steph closed her eyes, but images of the one and only time she'd seen the woman were imprinted in her mind, and now played back in vivid Technicolor.

'Who might she be, Steph?' Bob asked. 'Someone who could want to harm you or Fanny?''

'No!' Her protest was a cry of pain, and she began to shake. 'It's not her, and if it is, it's coincidence. It was all so long ago—I don't even know her second name.'

'If there's even a tiny chance she might know something about Fanny, we have to look into it,' Bob said, urging her to talk—not knowing why she didn't want to mention the woman's name, or her connection to the family.

'Harry thought it might be someone called Stella,' Brad said, and Steph, who'd thought things couldn't possibly get any worse, realised they could. It seemed as if the entire world was falling apart. 'Is that who you're thinking of?'

'Yes,' she said hoarsely, 'but I only met her once.'

Yet even as she said the words, she wondered. There'd been publicity about the hospital opening in the Brisbane papers as well as Summerland's local rag. Could Stella have seen it and been reminded of what might have been?

Brad, meanwhile, had moved away, and was talking on his mobile.

'Who is she?' Bob asked. 'Someone you both once worked with? Someone who knew Martin as well, so came to the opening of the hospital? But wouldn't that be natural? Not suspicious?'

Steph looked at Bob, then back to Brad, still busy on the phone. She took a deep breath. A choice between saving Fanny and hurting Bob was no choice at all.

'I'm sorry, Bob, I never intended you to know this,' she began, turning towards him so he could see how serious she was. 'But Stella was Martin's girlfriend.'

She shrugged as the burden of saying the words aloud landed, far too heavily, on her shoulders.

'I didn't know about her, but apparently they'd been involved before he married me. The relationship might have stopped for a while but, according to Stella, who visited me in hospital the day after Martin died, she was the only person he'd ever loved and they'd become lovers again within months of our marriage. In Stella's version of what happened, Martin only married me because he realised Harry was showing interest in me. While the three of us were just good friends, everything was fine, but when he thought Harry and I might get together, he felt he'd be cut out of the friendship.'

Aware Bob was staring at her like a man turned to stone, she shrugged again, then continued.

'I guess you should also know that, according to Stella, she wasn't the only woman he was playing around with. That's what hurt me so much when Martin died, Bob. The fact that he'd betrayed me, not just with Stella but with other women. And that he'd never really loved me! That hurt, too. I didn't tell you and Doreen because I didn't want to spoil your memory of him, but

I couldn't live with you any more, or hear you talk about how wonderful he was, when I was hurting so much.'

She brushed at the tears now rolling down her cheeks.

'Stella hated me—blamed me for Martin's death. She told me all of that in one short visit. But it was so long ago. Why would she wait till now to hurt me? It's impossible!'

'You say Harry knew this?' Bob's voice was as hoarse as hers had been, and Steph realised he was feeling the grief of losing his son all over again.

'Harry knew!' Steph said. 'I asked him about it when he visited later that day, and he admitted it. Said he'd kept quiet because he didn't want to hurt me, and Martin had kept promising to break off the relationship with Stella.'

She shook her head as the memories threatened to overwhelm her, adding more pain to the pain of Fanny's disappearance.

'This woman could be the one, then, if she hated you,' Bob said, turning to Brad and demanding to know what he was doing.

'We started tracking her down as soon as Harry mentioned her name last night,' Brad explained. 'I just phoned in to confirm Stephanie had recognised her as well. She's not at her flat at the moment. According to the hospital where she works, she's currently on leave. We've alerted all road patrols to look out for her car but, remember, she's only one of many people who were at the ceremony and we need to talk to all of them.'

He'd just finished explaining this when his phone rang again.

'I have to get back to the office,' he said, when the phone call was completed. 'I'll leave the video with you. If you could go through and put names to any of the other faces. Stella was number four, so just number them and write the name—or ''unknown''—against the numbers. One of my men will call for the video and list later.'

He stood up, and Steph stood with him—wanting to be where the action was.

'No! There's nothing new. I'm wanted back there on another matter, but I'll keep in touch. We'll do this carefully.'

Was Stella a lead or a false trail?

Steph wasn't sure.

She made coffee for herself and Bob, then started the video running again. Together they identified four more faces as staff members, and in the end had only two labelled as unknown. Now, as the policeman hadn't arrived to collect the tape, she ran it again, pausing on the face that might be Stella's.

Wondering whether or not to hope this woman was responsible for Fanny's disappearance.

On the hope side—surely someone who had loved him wouldn't harm Martin's child...

On the down side—Stella's confrontation with Steph all those years ago had been laced with such hatred she could harm Fanny to strike out at Steph...

Then there was the possibility they'd confronted right from the beginning—that a total stranger had taken her...

CHAPTER TEN

HARRY checked his patient, then talked to Ty about what they would be doing that day in preparation for the operation, and the following day during it. But his mind was only half on what he said, the rest of it desperate to discover a way to find Fanny, while on a deeper layer he agonised over what would happen to Steph if the unthinkable happened and they didn't find her beautiful child.

At this stage of his cogitation his lungs cramped, and he forced his mind back to his patient, explaining now what would happen in the days immediately after the op.

'Steph told me all about it. Have they found her little girl?'

Ty's note rekindled Harry's anxiety, but he fought it down and said firmly, 'No, but they will.'

Did positive thinking work? And how badly was it affected by the dread he also felt?

Once satisfied that Ty understood what was to happen to him, Harry checked that Rebecca was keeping things going in the office, then headed back to Steph's house, calling at the police station on the way for the most recent news.

'Did you know this Stella?' Brad asked.

Harry shrugged.

'Not well, but as a co-worker, yes, I guess so. She was a nurse in the O and G ward at the time Martin and I did a clinical term there. Steph was doing paediatrics at the time, I think.'

'Would she remember you?'

Harry frowned at Brad while he thought about the question.

'Yes, I suppose so. I mean, I recognised her, so maybe she'd recognise me—well, she would, if that *was* her at the ceremony, because all the specialists were introduced by name and we had to stand and kind of be acknowledged.'

'That could be useful,' Brad said. 'If we find her and there's a chance she has the child, she might be less freaked out by someone she knows.'

'Page me if you need me,' Harry told him, giving him the contact number for his pager. 'I'll call you back. That way we won't raise Steph's hopes unnecessarily.'

Brad nodded, then shook his head, and Harry knew what he was thinking. The longer this went on, the less chance there was of finding Fanny alive.

He left the building, and drove towards Steph's house, his heart heavy in his chest as he considered the situation. He'd come back to Summerland hoping he and Steph might stand a chance of finding happiness together. And once they'd met again that hope had become a possibility.

Oh, there'd been setbacks, but somehow he'd sensed he was getting closer to achieving his dream—that he, Steph and Fanny would somehow become a family. That he could make up for the hurt she'd suffered in the past and teach her to trust again.

But now?

Harry shook his head, thinking instead about Fanny—and Stella Spence, who'd been the cause of so much pain to Steph once before.

Could she be the cause again?

*   *   *

The day dragged on. Harry had returned at midday but with no news by late afternoon, he'd been paged and called away again, presumably to go to the hospital for the briefing with the other specialists involved in the operation. Steph thought of Ty, but couldn't feel her usual hope and apprehension for the young lad and what lay ahead of him. Her exhausted body and mind were so concentrated on Fanny's safety, an atom bomb exploding beside her would have failed to elicit a reaction.

At ten that evening, a young policeman arrived at the house.

'Brad sent me to tell you we've located Stella. She's in a motel near the beach at the southern end of Summerland. Long-range microphones have picked up television noise and what could be conversation masked by the TV. The motel owners thought she was alone when she checked in at about nine on Saturday night, but admit there could have been a child asleep in the car.'

Hope was hammering in Steph's heart as she heard the news, and she grasped the young man's arm, wanting to shake more information out of him.

'Apparently Stella told the owner she wanted to be left in peace,' he said. 'She explained she was a nurse on leave and all she wanted to do was sleep for a few days, but the owners have heard the television going most of the day, starting from children's programmes early in the morning.'

'If she checked in on Saturday evening, it fits. And Fanny loves TV, though I don't let her watch a lot of it,' Steph said, excited yet dreading that Fanny might not be with the woman. 'Why don't you just go in and see if Fanny's there?'

'Brad's watching the room. He's waiting until later.

It's safer if we go in when Stella's asleep. I'm here to collect you. We'll leave as soon as I get a message to say the light has gone out in the unit. You can sit in the car so if Fanny is there, we can give her straight to you.'

'If Fanny's there alive,' Bob muttered brokenly, and Steph turned on him.

'Of course she'll be alive. We've got to believe that, Bob! We have to have faith.'

She ran into Fanny's room and grabbed her bear, still sporting his bright ribbon bow-tie from the day he'd been to kindy. Then she picked up a blanket which had been on Fanny's cot when she'd been a baby. Clutching both these talismans, she returned to the living room.

'Let's go,' she said.

'It's too early,' the policeman protested.

'Then we'll sit outside. You must have other cars parked there, listening and keeping watch. We'll keep watch with them.'

She led the way to the car, the young man following, while Bob had the presence of mind to find her keys and lock the door behind them.

The motel was down a quiet side street, and on a Monday night had only two cars parked outside it. The lighting outside was dim, so the light shining from behind the curtain in the window of the fifth unit along threw a square of pale yellow on the path that ran along the front of the building.

'That's one of our cars ahead of us,' the policeman said, pointing to a car in the deep shadow of a huge fig tree. 'They'll wait about an hour after the light goes out,' he added, as Steph fought the urge to leap out of the car, race across the driveway, smash open the door and seize her daughter. Though tortured by anxiety, she still realised such an action could provoke Stella to harm her child.

If Stella had her child...

They sat in the darkness, seemingly for ever, while Steph's limbs grew chilled and heavy, matching the cold fear in her heart.

Then the square of yellow light disappeared, and she tensed.

'Soon,' the policeman said. 'They'll need to give her time to get properly to sleep.'

He turned to Steph.

'You realise she might not have Fanny.' He spoke soberly, reminding her this was an off-chance. 'She *could* be here on leave, tired after night duty, just wanting to sleep for a few days. And being in Summerland, maybe she just joined the crowd to see the opening of a hospital named after her lover.'

'I realise that,' Steph told him. 'But I feel this is right. I know it's stupid, but I can't help sensing Fanny's near.'

She squeezed Bob's hand.

'And alive.'

The next fifty minutes were interminable, then there was movement at the car in front, doors opening silently and dark figures walking in shadows towards the motel. Steph saw the black shadows of two back-up men move to the rear of the building, and two more figures, one a woman, fall in on either side of Brad.

The policeman had explained what they would do. Using a key he'd procured from the motel owner, Brad would unlock the door and turn on the light. Even if Stella woke immediately, the three policemen would be in the room, and if Fanny was there, she would be the main priority, the three law officers moving directly to cover her from any attack.

Steph didn't like to think about what form the attack might take, or about possible harm to the three people who would put their lives at risk to save her child.

If she was there...

As the threesome approached the building, light from the front office lit up their silhouettes.

'The tall one—that's not a policeman, it's Harry!' Steph gasped, as the shadows became people. 'Why's he there? What's he doing?'

She was clutching Bob's arm, and shaking with an unnamable dread, but before Bob could answer—if he'd had an answer—she saw the door of the unit they'd been watching open. As a light flashed on, it was Harry who went first into the room.

Steph closed her eyes and prayed, though for Harry this time, as well as Fanny.

The figures disappeared into the room, then she heard Brad's excited cry of, 'Bingo!'

It wasn't an arranged signal, but Steph knew what it meant. She was out of the car and racing across the driveway at the back of the motel, reaching the door of the unit as Harry came out, a small, blonde-headed bundle held snugly in his arms.

Steph snatched the burden from him, but even as she pressed Fanny close to her chest, she glared at the man who'd rescued her.

'You could have been killed,' she muttered angrily at him, then her gaze feasted on her child, scanning every inch of skin to assure herself it *was* Fanny and she was alive and well.

Fanny opened sleepy eyes and smiled.

'Oh, Mummy, you're back. I'm so glad. Stella is so boring. Did you see my picture on TV? Was it because I cut the ribbon they kept putting it on?'

She snuggled closer to Steph, who closed her eyes and gave thanks, not only for the safe return of her child but to Stella as well, who had somehow managed to make the whole ordeal boring rather than traumatic for her child.

Then the agony of the past few days caught up with her, and relief weakened her knees. She sagged and would have collapsed if Harry and Bob, both hovering by her side, hadn't caught her and helped her to the car.

The young policeman drove them home, where Bob picked up his car and departed, eager to tell Doreen the good news.

Determined to keep things as normal as possible for Fanny, Steph put her into her own bed, read her a story and watched her fall asleep before the first page was finished.

'Now, bed for you, too,' Harry said. 'I'll stay. I'll watch her.'

'You can't,' Steph told him, though she was now so tired she could barely talk. 'You have to sleep yourself. You're operating tomorrow.'

He reached out and grasped her shoulders, looking down into her eyes.

'I've asked someone else to do it,' he said.

'But you can't do that. You came home to do these operations—it was your dream, Harry.' Tiredness lifted enough for her to protest.

'Dreams don't mean much when you're faced with the reality we've all faced this last weekend, Steph,' he said gently, his dark eyes soft with anguish. 'It's a terrible thing for a man to realise he can't protect the woman he loves, but at least I could be here for you. I couldn't not do that. And I won't leave you now.'

He touched her softly on the cheek, then smoothed his

finger between her eyebrows where she knew frown marks must be settling in.

'Don't worry. As soon as you're rested, I'll catch up on a bit of sleep, then take over from the primary surgeon this afternoon. We'd worked out we'd need to do shifts.'

Steph knew she was too tired for her thoughts to be making sense, but she certainly wasn't worrying about Harry's part in Ty's operation. In fact, she wasn't sure what she was worrying about—but it had begun when she'd seen him walk into that motel room...

She woke with a start, leaping off the bed and racing to Fanny's room, seeing not her daughter but a tousled, slept-in bed that reassured her the previous night's events hadn't been a dream.

Fanny was in the lounge, sitting on Harry's knee while he brushed her hair.

'I got dressed all by myself, but I couldn't do my hair,' Fanny announced, and Steph felt tears rush into her eyes. Fanny was all right!

She lifted her daughter into her arms and hugged her, then, as Fanny announced she could get her own breakfast and departed to the kitchen, Steph turned to Harry.

'Thank you,' she said, smiling for what seemed like the first time in months.

'I don't need thanks, Steph. You know that.'

Harry stood up and she saw the tiredness in the way he moved, but when he took hold of her shoulders she felt his quiet strength, and when he looked into her eyes she saw the love he felt for her.

'I know you need to spend some time with Fanny right now,' he said gently. 'But when you're feeling more secure—when you've convinced yourself she's safe—would you take a little time to think about us?

About you and me and whether there's a future for us—together?'

He sighed then kissed her gently on the lips.

'I know Martin betrayed your trust, and this horrific incident has put further dents in it. I'd love to promise you'd never suffer unhappiness again, but there are no guarantees in this world, Steph. All I can promise is, whatever happens in the future, I love you and will always be there for you.'

He turned away before she could think of a reply—before she could explain that she was so mixed up right now that love was the last thing on her mind.

But when she thought over what he'd said, she realised Harry must have known that. He'd told her how he felt and was leaving the rest to her.

Steph spent the week at home, knowing Fanny needed to get back into her normal routine but unable to be far away from her, even going so far as to sit in her car outside the kindy, watching over the child she'd so nearly lost.

Rebecca reported regularly on Ty's progress. The operation had been a success, he was out of the ICU and doing really well. The test would come when the bandages came off and the lad tried to move his jaw.

Harry was seeing patients—busier than he'd expected to be because once Fanny had been found Bob had turned his attention back to work and had milked the 'free' operation for all the publicity he could get.

Inevitably, some of this spotlight shone on Harry, and referrals for facial surgery were coming in at a steady rate.

But as Steph's stress levels dropped, and life began to

fall back into its normal pattern, she began to wonder why Harry hadn't called or come to see them.

Because he left it up to you to make the next move, she reminded herself. He's offered you his love—and left you to decide if you want to take it.

Left you to decide if you trust that love…

She pondered it on the Friday—the first day she felt secure enough to leave Fanny at kindy and actually drive home. But not secure enough to get back into her work routine.

Brad had called on Wednesday evening. Stella had admitted seeing the publicity about the hospital opening. Apparently, she'd been four months pregnant by Martin when he'd died, but had lost the baby. The publicity brought back her pain and grief and loss, and with them an overwhelming sense of injustice.

She hadn't so much planned to kidnap Fanny as gone looking for an opportunity to do harm. She'd bought supplies so she could hole up in a motel somewhere, still thinking more of ruining the opening ceremony then getting away, not considering taking the child.

But Fanny had looked so like Martin that her control had broken. She'd followed the guests' cars to the Quayles' house, then had mingled with the guests. She'd stayed in the house with Martin many years earlier when his parents had been overseas, so knew her way around, and when she'd found Fanny sleeping, it had seemed so easy just to pick her up and carry her down the back stairs and out the door that led to the service gate.

Brad suspected she'd planned it more thoroughly than she admitted as her car had been parked near that exit, but she was adamant that taking Fanny had been a spur-of-the-moment decision.

In reply to Steph's question of what would happen to

Stella now, Brad had shrugged, explaining it would be up to the courts, but he guessed they would recommend a psychiatric evaluation.

Steph, now Fanny had been returned to her, felt pity for the woman who'd been cheated of everything she'd ever wanted. And though she'd vowed to put her bitterness and anger towards Martin behind her, she couldn't help but lay the blame for Stella's actions at his door.

And thinking of Martin, she *had* to think of Harry. To think about 'us', as he'd put it.

Was she ready to put her happiness into someone else's hands—her own and Fanny's happiness?

Was she ready to trust again?

Forget Harry, think about a job, she told herself when no answer to her queries about that part of her future popped obligingly into her head.

But it was still too soon to consider going back to work. She was, with difficulty, giving up her post outside the kindy, but leaving Fanny while she went to work seemed too big a hurdle to contemplate just yet.

Maybe in a little while…

Bob arrived that afternoon as she was still pondering the options. He was more understanding now, and though he hadn't pushed her to return to live with them, today's offer wasn't that far off.

'Let me pay off the house for you and give you an allowance,' he said. 'Then you won't have to work.'

'But I enjoy work,' she explained to him. 'And I need to do something. I can't sit at home on my own all day, worrying about Fanny. As well as going nuts myself, I'd probably do her irreparable psychological harm by being an over-protective mother.'

'Will you go back to work for Harry?'

Steph shrugged.

'I don't know if the job's still on offer,' she admitted. 'And, to be honest, women with dependent children aren't the most dependable of employees. Surgeons can't back out of an operation at the last minute, but if Fanny was sick, I might have to do just that.'

Bob nodded.

'Though Doreen could pick up a lot of the slack at times like that if you let her. I know she's been a weak reed to lean on since Martin's death, but Fanny's disappearance has changed all that. She hasn't touched a drop of alcohol, and she's doing volunteer work at the hospital.'

He touched Steph gently on the shoulder.

'She needs to be needed, Steph.'

This time it was Steph who nodded, but having Doreen available to mind Fanny if Tracy was at college made a range of jobs now possible.

Forget jobs and think about Harry!

In the end, she went to see him. Collecting Fanny herself from kindy then later leaving her with Tracy for the first time since her daughter's disappearance, Steph set off for the hospital.

First stop was the new, sparsely populated surgical ward to visit Ty, who was in good spirits and already moving his jaw experimentally, although it was still heavily bandaged.

Then on to Harry's rooms, where she hesitated before opening the door.

It was late enough for Rebecca and the new junior Rebecca had employed to have left, but the fact that the door was unlocked suggested Harry would still be there.

She hesitated outside the closed door of his consulting room.

'Harry?'

No answer, but she heard a shuffling sound, then the door opened and he was standing there.

'You look terrible,' she said, seeing the lines strain had etched in his face and the pain and tiredness in his eyes.

'Harry!' His name slipped out again, this time as a protest. 'What's wrong?'

He tried a smile but it was a dim, exhausted effort.

'It hasn't been the best week I've ever had, Steph,' he said, not moving to invite her in, not reaching out to touch her.

'Ty? Is it Ty? Are there complications?'

She was so anxious she reached out herself, grasping his forearm, feeling his muscles contract as if he'd flinched at her touch.

She took her hand away, then stared at it, wondering how a pale palm, four fingers and a thumb could cause offence.

Beyond Harry's shoulder she could see X-rays in the viewing boxes and, seeking a bit of normality in what had suddenly become an unreal situation, she stepped past him, saying, 'Are these Ty's? Are they the latest? Are you happy with the way things went?'

She knew he'd followed her into the room because the skin on her back was prickling with awareness of his presence.

'Very happy,' he said in a voice more suited to a funeral than a celebration of success. 'See here, where we pinned new bone, if you look closely you can see it's already starting to grow.'

He came closer to point to the section he wanted her to see, and her body throbbed with being so close, yet not close enough. Throbbed with uncertainty as well, because this Harry seemed completely oblivious to her as anything other than a fellow doctor.

She turned away from the films—she wasn't concentrating on what he was saying anyway—and rested her hands on his shoulders. Again she felt that stiffening, but she'd come to say things and wasn't going to be put off.

'Harry, I've thought about what you said—about us.'

'And?' he prompted, and she saw wariness in his eyes as if he feared bad news. 'Is there an us?'

'I think so,' she said softly, 'but it would help me be sure if you kissed me.'

She saw the veil of tiredness lift from his face and the glow of love light his eyes, then she was in his arms, clinging to him as if she'd been adrift on a wind-tossed sea for far too long.

Then his lips met hers and she gave in to the sheer bliss of being in Harry's arms—or kissing Harry.

A long time later they stopped for air, and she snuggled up against him.

'You're sure about this?' he said, his voice betraying a mix of awe and hope.

'Absolutely,' Steph said. 'That morning, after Fanny came back, you talked about guarantees. I'm not asking you for any guarantees. I've already figured out they're not possible. But loving you, and knowing you love me—that's enough for now. All last weekend, while Fanny was missing, I kept telling myself that getting her back would make my life complete. I thought it was all I could ever wish for.'

She studied Harry's face, so familiar—so dear.

'And getting her back was like a miracle. Even though I was still fearful, and obsessively over-protective, I could at least breathe normally again. Then, as the week progressed, I realised breathing wasn't enough. I was alive, but not really living, Harry. Believe me, I know the difference. I've been like that for nearly five years, and enough's enough.'

Harry's arms closed more tightly around her.

'There is one guarantee I can give, Steph,' he said, as his gaze roamed her face, feasting on the so-familiar features like a starving man on food. 'And that's my love. For you, for Fanny, for any other children we might one day have. My love is yours—I guarantee it.'

Then he bent his head and sealed the words with a kiss.

LIVE THE EMOTION

Modern Romance™
...seduction and
passion guaranteed

Tender Romance™
...love affairs that
last a lifetime

Medical Romance™
...medical drama
on the pulse

Historical Romance™
...rich, vivid and
passionate

Sensual Romance™
...sassy, sexy and
seductive

Blaze Romance™
...the temperature's
rising

27 new titles every month.

Live the emotion

MILLS & BOON®

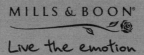

MILLS & BOON®

Live the emotion

Medical Romance™

STORMBOUND SURGEON by *Marion Lennox*

Joss Braden is bored. In fact he's out of Iluka as fast as his sports car can take him! But the bridge is down – there's no way on or off the headland. Suddenly Joss is responsible for a whole town's health, with only Amy Freye's nursing home as a makeshift hospital – and the chemistry between Joss and Amy is incredible!

OUTBACK SURGEON by *Leah Martyn*

Gorgeous Nick Tonnelli isn't just a high-flying surgeon, he's also a Sydney socialite. Outback GP Abbey Jones is charmed but confused when he makes his interest clear. The attraction between them is overwhelming, but will the glamorous surgeon really want a relationship with her?

THE DOCTOR'S ENGAGEMENT WISH
by *Gill Sanderson*

Erin Hunter had been the most beautiful girl at school – and like all the boys Josh Harrison had been in love with her. Now they have been reunited, while working as GPs, and Josh finds his attraction to Erin as strong as ever. But Erin isn't as carefree as he remembers, and he is determined to discover what has changed her...

On sale 4th July 2003

Available at most branches of WH Smith, Tesco, Martins, Borders, Eason, Sainsbury's and all good paperback bookshops.

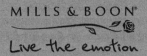

Medical Romance™

DR SOTIRIS'S WOMAN *by Margaret Barker*

Dr Francesca Metcalfe is the most gorgeous woman Dr Sotiris Popadopoulos has ever seen, and while they are working together on Ceres Island he hopes they will get to know each other better. But it seems that Francesca has chosen her career over having a family, and Sotiris has his young son who is need of a mother...

HER SPECIAL CHILD *by Kate Hardy*

One look at locum GP Tina Lawson and Dr Alex Bowen is smitten – surely she must feel the same? She certainly does – but she can't risk getting involved with Alex. Her son Josh needs all her love and attention.   But Alex is determined to prove passion will last – and two is better than one when it comes to caring for such a special little boy.

EMERGENCY AT VALLEY HOSPITAL
by Joanna Neil

Mistaking consultant Jake Balfour for a patient is bad enough – and if only he weren't so attractive... When Carys's sister is injured Jake's support is unexpected – but ever since her troubled childhood Carys has sworn off men. Could Jake be the man to change her mind?

On sale 4th July 2003

FREE
4 BOOKS
AND A SURPRISE GIFT!

We would like to take this opportunity to thank you for reading this Mills & Boon® book by offering you the chance to take FOUR more specially selected titles from the Medical Romance™ series absolutely FREE! We're also making this offer to introduce you to the benefits of the Reader Service™ —

- ★ FREE home delivery
- ★ FREE monthly Newsletter
- ★ FREE gifts and competitions
- ★ Exclusive Reader Service discount
- ★ Books available before they're in the shops

Accepting these FREE books and gift places you under no obligation to buy; you may cancel at any time, even after receiving your free shipment. Simply complete your details below and return the entire page to the address below. *You don't even need a stamp!*

YES! Please send me 4 free Medical Romance books and a surprise gift. I understand that unless you hear from me, I will receive 6 superb new titles every month for just £2.60 each, postage and packing free. I am under no obligation to purchase any books and may cancel my subscription at any time. The free books and gift will be mine to keep in any case.

M3ZED

Ms/Mrs/Miss/Mr ....Initials ....
BLOCK CAPITALS PLEASE

Surname ....

Address ....

....

....Postcode ....

Send this whole page to:
UK: FREEPOST CN81, Croydon, CR9 3WZ
EIRE: PO Box 4546, Kilcock, County Kildare (stamp required)

Offer valid in UK and Eire only and not available to current Reader Service subscribers to this series. We reserve the right to refuse an application and applicants must be aged 18 years or over. Only one application per household. Terms and prices subject to change without notice. Offer expires 30th September 2003. As a result of this application, you may receive offers from Harlequin Mills & Boon and other carefully selected companies. If you would prefer not to share in this opportunity please write to The Data Manager at the address above.

Mills & Boon® is a registered trademark owned by Harlequin Mills & Boon Limited.
Medical Romance™ is being used as a trademark.